THE SQUIRE OF
BOR SHACHOR

Also by Chaim Bermant

The Second Mrs. Whitberg

THE SQUIRE OF BOR SHACHOR

a novel
by
Chaim Bermant

ST. MARTIN'S PRESS   NEW YORK

Copyright © 1977 by Chaim Bermant
All rights reserved. For information, write:
St. Martin's Press, Inc., 175 Fifth Ave.,
New York, N.Y. 10010.
Manufactured in the United States of America
Library of Congress Catalog Card Number: 76-62572

Library of Congress Cataloging in Publication Data
Bermant, Chaim I
  The Squire of Bor Shachor.
  I. Title.
PZ4.B522Sq3 [PR6052.E63] 823'.9'14 76-62752
ISBN 0-312-75442-6

Contents

Chapter 1

The Natives are Friendly

Dear Berthold,

Well, here we are. I can't quite believe it myself, but there's the sun outside to prove it, and the blue skies, and the palm-trees. As long as we were in hotels and furnished rooms I had a vague feeling that we were merely playing, and that one morning I would turn to Celeste, or she to me, and say, well, the fun is over, it's time to return to England and reality. Once we bought the house, however, that was more or less that; we had plighted our troth. And now that we have finally moved in, our marriage to Israel is consummated.

No doubt you think we're crazy. Everybody else does. Celeste and I were unpacking this evening when she stopped for a moment and said: 'You know Henry, we are mad, aren't we?' And I said: 'Harmlessly so, I hope. It's not the sort of thing they can lock you up for.' 'I'm not so sure,' she said.

But of course it's her fault that we're here in the first place; at worst I'm an accessory before the fact. We were here last year (as we have been almost every year) and I had my usual grumbles about the inefficiency, the service, the hustle, the rudeness. England may not be the most efficient place on earth, but English inefficiency is relaxed and cheerful while inefficiency here comes with loud voices and sweated brows. I suppose it is a matter of choosing between sloth and incompetence, and incompetence, if the more forgiveable, is the more trying. The slightest transaction involves one in turmoil, and, as Celeste said to me, there's no point in grumbling unless you're prepared to do something about it.

'What can I do?' I said, 'we're only visitors.' 'Well, we can jolly well stop here for a start,' she said, 'and bring some civilisation to this place.' 'For good?' I said. 'For good,' she said. So here we are for better or for worse.

We chose Bor Shachor because property round here is not too expensive and, well, for sentimental reasons. We were here on our honeymoon in 1935 (or was it 1936, I never could remember dates), when Matthew was District Commissioner, and we fell in love with the place. It was known as Quol-boyeh then (does the name ring a bell now?), Bor Shachor being the new Jewish addition.

The actual name of the town is Be'er Hashachar – it is, I believe, called after some Zionist dignitary who is not other-wise remembered – but it has been corrupted to Bor Shachor which, I am told, is the Hebrew for Black Hole and which, if first impressions are anything to go by, is not an inappro-priate name. Little remains of the old Arab town, but happily that little includes perhaps half a dozen good stone houses of which this, which we are calling The Limes (we have limes growing in the garden, and a fig tree, but I can't imagine anyone calling their place The Figs, can you?), is one, or was one before the builders moved in.

The builders moved in a week after we exchanged con-tracts and should have been out by October. It is now March and Celeste is wondering whether we should charge them rent. I am not sure if they are Jews or Arabs, for most of the Jews round here look like Arabs and even where they speak Hebrew it sounds like Arabic, though in truth I know so little of either language that they both sound Greek to me. The contractor whose name is Patakos (Celeste calls him Dick Turpin), a short, red-faced man with blue eyes and gold teeth, is Jewish. He knows only two English words, money and soon, but finds them enough to get by with. I consulted Matthew about the possibility of taking legal action, but all the advice he could offer was, *never* have anything to do with lawyers, it's always cheaper to pay up. He's a bit past it, poor Matthew, rarely stirs from Jerusalem and drinks rather a lot.

He's only in his early seventies (isn't he?), but, between ourselves, he's in worse shape than poor Father (not a word to Father, though – it would upset him). And to think that if the Empire had continued for another year or two he might have been Governor General of some place or other, and a knight. I suppose the fact that he's only a CBE and has never quite made it to the top is the reason why he is the way he is. It's a pity he never married, for he is getting quite derelict and needs someone to look after him.

The natives are friendly. We were at first taken for tourists and people kept asking us when we were coming to stay. When we said we were staying, they asked what I did, and how much I was earning. I said I was doing nothing. 'That's what everybody does,' I was told, 'but what should you be doing when you're doing nothing?' and I explained I was retired, which is an unfamiliar concept, for round here the only known way of retiring is to drop dead whereas I show passing signs of being alive.

We have made a number of acquaintances, though the only people we know really well tend to be expatriates, or what Matthew used to call 'the Government House set', fairly well-to-do Americans, Britons, and South Africans who wander around the place with the mildly distraught look of people who have been landed on the wrong shore, and I am not really convinced that we have landed on the right shore ourselves, but time will tell.

In the house next door there lives the Chicago family Gittleson, consisting of a thin, worried-looking husband, a rather less thin worried-looking wife, and a pair of thin worried-looking children in ragged jeans, brightly coloured plimsolls and faded sweat-shirts. All are long-haired, save the husband, and all wear glasses, save the wife.

Mrs G, who is garbed like her children and who, one imagines, could look fairly attractive in a dress (and perhaps even more so out of one) has a shrill eagerness which I find slightly unnerving. She accosted Celeste in the street one morning with the greeting: 'Welcome to the club!' When Celeste blinked, she added: 'the optees club, I mean – you are here to opt out of the rat-race, aren't you?' As Celeste

wouldn't know the rat-race from the St Leger, she gave a suit-
ably non-committal reply.

Did I mention that we have a gardener? It's something of
an extravagance for we haven't much of a garden and what
there is of it is mostly rock and what we really need is a
quarry-man, but we engaged him without knowing we had,
and certainly without any intention of doing so. He came by
one afternoon and offered to put the garden in shape and I
said that that was something I hoped to do myself, which I
think is a reasonably polite way of saying no, but it may have
been too polite. We were wakened early the next morning by
the sound of iron on stone, and there, below, he was at work
in the garden. His name is Humphry. His appearance doesn't
quite go with the name, for he is a squat, swarthy Moroccan
with one eye, a blue chin and a neck like a tree-trunk. He has
a reasonable command of English which he picked up from
American soldiers during the war (one hopes he picked up
nothing worse) and it was they who christened him Humphry.
Apart from looking after the garden, he also cleans the car
and has offered to make good the damage which, he says,
builders round here always leave in their wake. 'Everybody
make work for everybody else,' he said, 'doctors for doctors,
lawyers for lawyers, builders for builders.' Celeste in a rash
moment asked him if he knew where to get free-range eggs.
An hour later he was back with six eggs under his hat and,
for good measure, he pulled a half-asphyxiated chicken from
his pocket which he said was a free-range hen. He has also
offered to find us free-range beef, free-range mutton and free-
range whisky. It would perhaps be too much to describe
Humphry as a treasure, but whether we like it or not, he has
become part of our household.

We had thought of waiting a bit before looking around for
a suitable synagogue, but in the meantime the synagogue has,
so to speak, come to us. Yesterday morning a robust-looking
man with large teeth and a long beard dropped in, introduced
himself as Rabbi Mittwoch, Chief Rabbi of Bor Shachor, and
hoped that he would see something of us in his synagogue.
Hardly had he gone, when a shortish portly man appeared,
likewise bearded, who announced himself as Rabbi Selah,

Chief Rabbi of Bor Shachor, and hoped that he too would see something of us in his synagogue. I later asked Humphry how many Chief Rabbis there were in Bor Shachor and he said : 'In Bor Shachor everybody is chief.'

Our furniture should have been here by now but it is still on the high seas (if not under them) and we shall never feel quite at home until we are in our own beds. We hope, however, to have settled down sufficiently by the end of the month to think of being back in England in time for Father's hundredth birthday. How is he, by the way? Have you made up your mind on what form the celebrations should take? Presumably they'll be in Fetlock and not in London. Matthew has threatened to come, provided we pay his fare, but I'm a little afraid he may disgrace us (and I'm not only thinking of his drinking habits).

Do write. The children, as you may imagine, never do. They phone us from time to time, but only to apologise for not writing, and tell us very little. And Rodney doesn't even phone, and when he does he reverses the charges. I fear that he may have the makings of another Matthew. In the case of Matthew, at least, there was an Empire to absorb him. What am I to do with Rodney? Celeste says that I worry too much, but if she doesn't and I shouldn't, who will?

Yours,
Henry

P.S. I wonder if I could bother you to send me a substantial packet of Bassett's Liquorice Allsorts. One cannot get them here for love nor money (and certainly not for love) and, as you know, there is no other sweetmeat I care for.

P.P.S. Do you think Bassett's might grant me a franchise to manufacture allsorts locally?

Dear Gerald,

You upbraid me for sending you carbons of my letters to Berthold, but you should be grateful that I send you anything at all, seeing that you never take the trouble to answer them, and sending even a carbon is not the effortless matter you think it is. Nothing here comes without aggravation. I went to the post office to ask about the airmail rates to America and, after standing in the queue for half an hour, found that I had been waiting at the wrong counter. This is a country of specialists and if you want a postal order you stand at one counter, if you want stamps it's another, a cable and it's a third, an express-letter a fourth, and if you want all four of these things you can reckon to be in the post office for two days and a night. As a matter of fact there's been a go-slow this week, though I don't know how they can tell for I can't recall ever seeing a go-fast.

Your cable suggests a certain anxiety to hear from me, so here you have an original letter. Dare one hope that it will elicit a reply? (It is, by the way, something of an extravagance to send cables to Israel on Friday. Yours must have got here sometime after lunch, by which time the post office is shut, and it remains shut – even for cables -- throughout the Sabbath. It was in fact finally delivered with the morning post – which comes in the afternoon – on Sunday. It would have been almost as quick to write. Besides which, WHAT THE HELL GIVES QUERY is not an un-ambiguous message.)

We are on the whole enjoying ourselves here, though our stay has not been one unbroken spasm of pleasure, and in fact I have probably suffered more aggravation in the past few months than in the whole of my life in England, but that may of course be due to the fact that I am now retired and I have more time to get aggravated about my aggravations. Also in London one could escape to one's home from the frustrations of the office, whereas here my frustrations begin and end at home, for our builders, of whom you may have read in a previous letter (sorry, carbon) are still with us and I am beginning to wonder whether we shall have to regard them as one of the permanent fixtures of the place, and learn to live with them like bad plumbing or poor insulation. Yet the fact remains – one does not carry the aggravations of the one day over to the next. One awakes each morning amid blue skies and sunshine to a new account ever hopeful that things will go better, though, of course, they never do. All of which should tell you that I haven't changed with the change of climate and that, as Celeste puts it, I still like a jolly old grumble, and there is no better place to have it.

Are you still interested in finding a small place in Israel? There is a villa a few doors from us standing empty. It is of solid stone, with a spacious courtyard and I believe about twenty rooms, which is not my idea of small, but it may be yours. Shall I make inquiries? Matthew tells me it was built by the local pasha to house his harem. I do not add this by way of inducement, but I think it could fairly be called a house of character. The drawback to having a house of that size, however, is that relatives abhor a vacuum (especially in Israel) and I need hardly remind you that we have a very large family.

I take it you will be in England for Father's centenary celebrations. Couldn't you stop in here on the way and see the place for yourself? In any case we would like to see you, and, if not you, then at least Alice and the children.

Has Berthold written (or spoken) to you about Gwendoline? He asked me if I knew of anyone suitable in Bor Shachor. I said no one either he or I (or, I dare say, you) would care to have as a brother-in-law, but then I have only been here a few months. You've been in America for over forty years. Can't you think of someone? It is March, a time when even not such a young woman's fancy turns to thoughts of love, and, as you know, poor Gwendoline's fancy rarely turns to anything else. People often wonder why she isn't married. She is after all of good family, not without money, well educated, accomplished, well read and widely travelled. Her face is not her fortune, but I know of many plain women who have made very satisfactory marriages, and if her temper is not of the sweetest she has good cause to be sour, and in fact she can be perfectly charming when she is prepared to make the effort. She is, of course, choosy, which she has every right to be, but I doubt if she has a right to be as choosy as she is and she is not getting younger, while the family is getting poorer. She was feeling a little sorry for herself when we left England, poor child, and tended to be a prey to a whole host of illnesses large and small. Marriage may not be the panacea we Jews think it is, but it

would, I think, cure her of many of her complaints, the most
severe of which is being single. It is, alas, too late for her to
make anyone a good mother, but she could still make someone
a good wife. Isn't there an eligible male among your friends,
acquaintances, suppliers, employees? Do try.

Celeste is well, kept vibrant by her daily battles with Patakos and others and I, in spite of my grumbles, have never felt
better. The jolt of a drastic change does, I think, help one to
shed a few years. In Isleworth, especially after my retirement,
I had the cosy feeling one gets about four on a winter's afternoon, of darkness gradually drawing in on one, and it is all
very comforting, except that, of course, the darkness I speak
of is not followed by a new day. Coming here has given us (or
at least me – Celeste didn't quite need one yet) a new lease of
life. Matthew said it's all illusory but, as he added, an illusion
sustained is almost as good as reality. He sustains more than
a few illusions himself, poor man, and I need hardly add with
what he sustains them. Who said Jews don't drink? Of course
Matthew has never been particularly Jewish, or at least he
doesn't look it, which is perhaps why he got so far in the
Colonial Service. On the whole he can hold his drink, or
rather his drink holds him, for he becomes more upright,
colour floods into his face, his eyes glow, and at such times he
recovers something of his handsome looks. The one thing
which gives him away is his voice which deepens till it acquires
the crackling sound of tin foil, and he becomes almost totally
unintelligible, which is a blessing for the things he can say at
such times are not fit for civil or, indeed, uncivil ears. The
other is that drink is expensive, so that his money doesn't run
to anything else and he is, I'm afraid, beginning to look
decrepit. Celeste says that he has the sort of bearing that can
make decrepitude even stylish, but I don't see it that way, and
he troubles me.

The other nigger in the ointment (or is it fly in the wood-
pile?) is dear Rodney. I suppose that one is entitled to a dud
in the family, especially where one has been the family dud
oneself, and perhaps with William and Stanley doing so well I
should forget about Rodney and relax, but the boy does have
potential, and I certainly cannot avoid the feeling that there

is something in him yearning to be fulfilled. I only wish I knew what it was. Alice has suggested that it might do him good to come to New York for a bit. Do you think so? It's the 'bit' part which worries me. He has been everywhere for 'a bit' and got nowhere.

Love to Alice and the children,

Yours,
Henry

Dear Gwendoline,

It was good to hear from you, especially as Berthold mentioned that you had been in indifferent health. We would, of course, be delighted to have you here on a visit. Unfortunately the builders are still here and our furniture isn't, and the house which was barely habitable when we bought it, is, thanks to the efforts of Mr Patakos and his merry men, almost totally uninhabitable. When I complained to Patakos that we were in constant danger of being killed by falling masonry, he offered to lend me a steel helmet and, as a matter of fact, Celeste goes about her work in my old Home Guard helmet which, for some reason, I must have packed in my hand luggage. Happily the weather has been pleasant and there is something to be said, on these balmy April nights, for having a view of the heavens through one's bedroom ceiling.

Bor Shachor bears little relation to the Quolboyeh you visited when Matthew was DC. It has changed even more than Matthew. What was a large village is now a largish town, with about forty thousand inhabitants. The 'old' families came here from Germany in the thirties; the rest, who seem to be from everywhere, arrived in the past decade or two. It has a reasonably good shopping centre, including a large supermarket, but it isn't quite Knightsbridge, and as Celeste observed after our first outing: 'What Israel needs is Harrods.' We used to buy most of our groceries from a small corner shop, but the proprietor has an unfortunate habit of picking his nose and we have become more or less reconciled to the supermarket in the centre of town.

There are two or three cinemas in the place, seven or eight

synagogues, including a sizeable one by the municipal park, of which I have become a member. There is also a waterless swimming pool which I jokingly suggested was for people who couldn't swim, but there is apparently more to it than that. Bor Shachor has had a succession of scorching summers and it was decided to build a swimming pool, against the objections of the religious elements who feared that the provision of a pool for semi-clad beings would give rise to all sorts of lewd behaviour and that Bor Shachor would become another Sodom. The pool, however, took time building (Patakos must have been the contractor) and before it was complete there was a municipal election. The ruling Workers' Party lost its overall majority and needed the religious vote to stay in power, and so a compromise was arranged. The pool was completed, but it has been left dry.

There are few buildings of any distinction left in town. What Matthew called the Residency has been demolished, but the large building next to it which he nicknamed the Seraglio (and which, according to legend, was originally built for the harem of the local pasha) is still intact, though it is not in an ideal state of preservation. It overlooks our house and I'm a little nervous of the uses to which it might be put, though I have been assured it will be used neither as a school, nor as a youth club nor for any other purpose associated with children, for I am reaching an age when the only young people I can tolerate are my own grandchildren, and them for strictly limited periods. I am particularly nervous of the local children for they are very bright, very lively, very noisy and very insolent and will never accept reproof even from someone of my age, without answering back. Parenthood must be martyrdom here, though nothing comes with ease.

I recently went to open a current account at a local bank and I was directed by one clerk to another clerk, who sent me to a third, who gave me a sheaf of forms to fill out in triplicate which I then had to present to a fourth, who stamped one and directed me to a colleague on another floor, who stamped another and who then directed me to someone else, who eventually relieved me of the sum I wished to deposit, who in turn directed me to a young lady, who handed me a further form and eventually I was presented with a cheque book. The whole transaction took about an hour and a half – and that was to put money in! I daren't think what one may have to go through to take money out.

For a town of its size Bor Shachor has a remarkable number of bookshops. There is Steinmatzky's, the W. H. Smith of Israel. We get our English papers there, but it is too brisk and businesslike a place for browsing, and I have discovered a dusty little nook piled high with ancient tomes belonging to a Mr Gershowitz, a dusty little man with a snuff-stained moustache who looks as if he might have crawled out of one of his books, and he seems to be more interested in reading his stock than selling it. Nothing is stacked in any particular order, and it's more of a literary lucky dip than a shop, but I did find four of the six volumes of an early edition of Pepys's *Diary*. Gershowitz has assured me that he has the other two volumes somewhere in his place, if not in the shop, then in his flat above, or the cellar below, and that he will deliver them as soon as he finds them, which, however, may take a year or two. There is little light in the place and a heavy suspension of the decomposing souls of books and I am amazed how Gershowitz has survived in the atmosphere without some sort of breathing apparatus. There is also a bookshop, not unlike Gershowitz's, dealing exclusively in holy writ, and another dealing exclusively in unholy writ. It is tucked away in a back street and few people knew about it until some local zealot organised a demonstration against it. Now there is a constant crowd of small boys milling around it and it has branched out into the mail-order trade (rumour hath it that the zealot who led the demonstration is a brother-in-law of the proprietor).

Books, incidentally, are by no means confined to the bookshops round here, for there is no strict demarcation of trades. One can buy haberdashery in the hardware shop, hardware in the haberdasheries and books almost everywhere. The only shopkeepers who limit themselves to the goods indicated by their signs are the chemists, and they take a professional pride in limiting themselves strictly to pharmaceuticals, for chemists are regarded here, and indeed regard themselves, as quasi-doctors and form the mainstay of the local intelligentsia.

I recently popped into our local chemist for a bottle of aspirins, and he asked what for. My first reaction was to tell him to mind his own business, but he seemed to be showing legitimate professional interest and I told him that I had a headache.

'Where?'

'In the head.'

'But where in the head?'

'All over.'

'Do you have it often?'

'No, not very.'

And so, what was intended as a hurried call developed into a consultation at the end of which I came away with a packet of stomach powders instead of the aspirins. I am not sure that they've helped, but then the aspirins don't always help either and it is reassuring to know that one has in one's local chemist more than a shopkeeper anxious for a quick sale. He dresses like a surgeon in white coat with buttons at the side of the neck and exudes so much ether and self-assurance that I would cheerfully entrust my appendix to him.

I was not too happy about the tone of Berthold's last letter. He is too ready to assume burdens without working out the consequences and he sounded distinctly troubled. Has Father been difficult again, or is it business worries? He insists on staying on the board because, I suppose, it gets him out of the house and away from Father, but an ailing business can be even more troublesome than an ageing parent. It's alright for Martha to say a man should be in harness till he drops, but she is twenty years younger than him, besides which, she has never been in harness.

Celeste has had an attack of the usual things she gets whenever she goes abroad, but in more violent form. She insisted on an English doctor, as she always does when abroad (though in Isleworth, I may tell you, our National Health doctor is a Punjabi Sikh) and Matthew by chance happened to know one living a few streets away from him in Jerusalem. They arrived together in the early hours of the morning in a tiny wreck of a car, and the doctor seemed to be in no better shape than his vehicle. There was something uncomfortably familiar about

the man, and it was not the fact that he suffered palsy of the
hands and dropsy of the legs, and I said to Matthew, wasn't
he the chap Fogel who left London in a great hurry, and for
no apparent cause shortly before the war? And he said, Jove,
you have got a good memory. But it was too late for he had
already treated poor Celeste by then and she came out in con-
vulsions and blisters, and if it was not for our gardener, who
happens – apart from anything else – to be a dab hand with
a stomach pump, I might have been a widower by now. Fogel
fled as soon as he had administered his medicine (and his bill)
but Matthew is still with us and I suspect he recommended
Fogel in the first place to get a lift.

I have not been too well myself. While Celeste was ill our
gardener did the cooking and he prepared a dish which he
said was his mother's special, a spoonful of which left me
without voice for two days and without an appetite for a
week.

Matthew has pronounced our place unfit for human habita-
tion, which has not stopped him from inhabiting our front
room, and emptying the entire contents of our makeshift cocktail cabinet (a wooden box, in fact) including a much
cherished bottle of ginger wine which Celeste had brought all
the way from London.

I mention all this not to excite your sympathy, but because
I am told you're upset that we have been here six months
now and haven't asked you to stay with us. First of all, as my
sister, you shouldn't have to wait for an invitation. Matthew
doesn't hesitate to come here at every opportunity and make
himself a nuisance without any invitation whatever. Secondly,
our circumstances – meaning the state of our house, our
health and our nerves – are such as to make it impossible for
us to do any entertaining whatever. On the other hand I
appreciate your need to get away from home from time to
time. We hope to have the builders, and perhaps also
Matthew, out by the end of this month, and if you should care
to come down for a visit any time after May, we shall, of
course, be delighted to have you.

I appreciate your remarks about Rodney. It is true that
everybody loves him, but then he is not everybody's child and

he has been an almost constant source of vexation to Celeste and me. Of course he's not a 'bad' boy, for as you say he is incapable of doing anything wicked, but neither is he capable of doing anything useful in spite of the fact that he did well at school, and, had he cared to exert himself, might have done very well at university. Instead, he came away with a pass degree in a subject I had never heard of – 'Human Relations', I think it was – from a place which wasn't even a university. It was, as Celeste put it, 'neither red-brick, nor white-tile, but black hole'. I am never quite sure what he's doing because he is never quite sure himself, though I once discovered that he was a social worker of sorts, after a derelict couple he was supposed to be looking after came to tell me they were worried about his appearance and health and they were rather afraid he was falling into bad company.

I have of course asked him to join us here. As you know he lived on a kibbutz for a year or so, and I thought he liked Israel, but he wrote back to say that he would never set foot here 'until the Zionists abandoned their Empire'. I am not sure what he meant by that, but then I am not sure what he means by most of the things he says and young people nowadays seem to use a private language of their own. He is, of course, only twenty-two (or is it twenty-three?) and may yet meet a girl who could bring him to his senses, but if you should in the meantime be able to keep an – what's female of avuncular? – eye on him, both Celeste and I would be very grateful.

Celeste sends her love. She is still in bed, poor dear, but hopes to be up and about in another day or so.

Your loving brother,

Henry

Celeste Darling,

I hope you got the message.

I am sorry not to be with you. I had, as you can imagine, every intention of coming, but the car which (as you know) is being serviced and which (as you know) should have been ready last week, will be ready tomorrow, and here I am at home and immobilised. (If the car is not ready by tomorrow I intend to take a taxi and send the garage the bill.)

I must say that the house seems very large and empty without you – the sort of feeling we had in Isleworth after the children got married. We got used to it, of course, but I doubt if I could ever get used to Bor Shachor on my own. I suppose, given familiar company, no place is wholly strange.

You seemed, as you were driven off, even more worried about me than I was about you – as if I was the patient. How will I manage, you kept asking, how will I manage, which, if I may say so, my dear, is a little unlike you, for I was always the worrier of the family, and I took your anxiety as further proof of your ill health; I am, in fact, managing very well and am neither as old nor as helpless as I look and even with Humphry to help me I could probably cope very well, but in fact I have never even been given a chance to try.

This may seem a fairly harsh place in normal circumstances, but if word gets around that one is in difficulties one is laid under siege. The door-bell hasn't stopped ringing since you left and when it did stop it was because a member of the Patakos troupe had short-circuited the electricity. People wanted to know the nature of your complaint, how long you had it and who did you get it from, in other words, was it hereditary or contagious, did you have an operation, would you be having an operation? One lady showed me her scar, another recommended her surgeon, a third – and she a complete stranger – asked if you were having your change of life. Our chemist swears by something called Lupescu's stomach powder, a canister of which I shall be bringing with me, and there has been a constant succession of people bearing advice, oranges, bananas, comfort and fresh figs, and our friendly neighbourhood, nose-picking grocer came round with a box of eggs. A lady from two streets away offered to do my shopping, and before I could explain that I had none to do, she had vanished and reappeared with a box of assorted groceries. Rabbi Mittwoch has offered up prayers for your recovery in his synagogue, and Rabbi Selah in his (so that if you should have a relapse, you will know who to blame). The latter has also brought me a small psalter to read last thing at night before going to bed, as a mark of his affection and respect and to show that we were both forgiven.

He is unhappy at the fact that we have given our patronage exclusively to Mittwoch's synagogue.

'Why?' he demanded almost tearfully, 'you never come to me?'

I explained that we were Ashkenazim.

'Your wife also?'

'My wife also.'

'But she is old English.'

'Not very old English, which is to say, not Sephardi Old English.'

He dismissed all that as a detail. Ancestors, he said, were not important, it's the soul that counts, and he could see by your face and mine that we have Sephardi souls. Doesn't that make you feel better, my dear? He also added that while he had no wish to cast aspersions on the integrity of his Ashkenazi colleague, Rabbi Mittwoch, 'though a great scholar and a saintly man', had a lax temperament, and a habit of not wanting to see what he might find displeasing (who does?), that he is more of a politician than a Rabbi, that he only got his job because his brother-in-law was married to the sister of the secretary of the Holy Alliance Party, that he had, contrary to Jewish law, allowed a man with deformed genitals to get married in his synagogue, and that if it wasn't for him (i.e. Selah) Judaism would be dead in Bor Shachor, and that we would discover this for ourselves once we had settled down.

Mrs Gittleson (whom you and I shall have to learn to call Nicky, short for Veronica) is an angel. She has done my shopping, cooked my meals (I have banished Humphry from the kitchen for life) and even offered to do my laundry. I had hoped that Matthew might be driven away by hunger, but the effect of her hospitality has been to extend his stay indefinitely. She invited us both to a formal dinner last night and, presumably for Matthew's benefit, had a blonde American divorcée at table and the conversation and Coca-Cola flowed freely till Matthew asked in a loud voice if there was such a thing as a brandy in the house. By chance there was, and 'ere the evening was out, it ceased to be, especially after Matthew persuaded Mr Gittleson (hereinafter to be known as Gary) to have a drop. M, I'm afraid, paid very little attention to the divorcée and a great deal – some might say excessive – attention to Nicky, and I'm not sure you're right that he has no real interest in women (was it you who said that it had something to do with his civil service training?). Nicky can look very attractive once she gets out of her jeans and into a dress, for she has a beautiful neck and shoulders and a flawless white skin and Matthew kept hovering over her and snorting brandy fumes into her cleavage.

They all, of course, asked after you, and Nicky in particular was anxious to know if and when she could visit you and what she could bring. I told her that you hated to be caught at a disadvantage, which is to say, on your back in bed, and that you were not all that enthusiastic to have even me as a visitor. She said she couldn't believe it and that she would die if she spent a morning without seeing a new face, to which Matthew interjected: 'Rather surprising in the circumstances that you've been married to the same man all these years.'

'She hasn't,' said Gary, 'I'm number two,' in a way which suggested that number three couldn't be far behind.

I do miss you, my dear. I liked their company but I would have liked it more if you had been there. I don't think I'm unsocial but it's so long since I've been out on my own in the evening that on those occasions when I do go I feel oddly vulnerable and incomplete, and, I suppose, slightly dour. I had hardly anything to say for myself.

The conversation was mostly about health, your ill health and their good health. Nicky said that the difference between the English and Americans is that the former go in for cures, and the latter for prevention, and she showed me her medicine cupboard – a veritable pharmacy replete with everything short of Lupescu's stomach powder. They have potions before meals and after meals and during meals and first thing in the morning and last thing at night. 'The thing to do,' said Nicky, 'is to make your interior inhospitable to foreign bodies,' to which Matthew crackled something which was thankfully inaudible.

Gary was in advertising and by the look and size of their house, and the number and size of their cars, he must have done very well out of it. I am not sure what an advertising man (especially an American advertising man) should look like, but I wouldn't have expected someone quite as donnish and subdued as Gary. You get the feeling he'd break into tears if you said boo to him. He has an English degree from Yale University and, as soon as his Hebrew is good enough, he hopes to become a school teacher. The poor man will be eaten alive. Their two boys are rather gifted and after dinner we were entertained to *un moment musicale*, with Gary at the piano, the two boys on violins and Nicky on the flute. They played well though the pleasure was marred a little by Matthew who fell fast asleep and snored loudly throughout the performance. Their whole establishment doesn't go with what one knows of America, but then what I know of America is derived largely from my knowledge of Gerald, who, I must remind myself, was born in Britain and educated in a good British public school and one should not perhaps blame America for the ogre he has become.

We've been having a heat-wave with temperatures of a hundred in the shade. The Gittlesons have air-conditioners whining away in every room, but in fact these old, stone house are well built to withstand heat, and even if they weren't I'm not sure if I wouldn't rather have the heat than the noise. Besides which, I rather enjoy the heat. The air quivers and dances, distant prospects become hazy and one is overcome with a sort of snug lethargy. It is, I should imagine, no pleasure to be at work in such temperatures, but it is ideal for us ancient refugees from the cold. I lunch on a plate of cheese and chilled white wine, and then sink into sleep with *The Times* opened in front of me, the mind a haze of sunny fantasies. The evenings are as hot as the days, and there is no relief even in the night, when the air is so balmy one can almost grasp it. Everything has a tired, weary sound to it, even the television echoing from the balconies, and noises seem suspended in the air before fading away. I find it difficult to sleep at night, but as I sleep well during the day I can hardly complain. Yesterday I rose at midnight for a long walk round

Bor Shachor and found half the town taking the night air in their pyjamas.

There has been a hitch in the plans for the centenary celebrations. Father insists that he is not a day over ninety-two, which would have meant that he sired Berthold (who is seventy-eight) when he was thirteen. When B pointed this out Father sank under his blankets and out of sight, and now refuses to see or speak to anyone and even Miss Naysmith, who usually manages to humour him, has proved unavailing. It is all very trying for Berthold, and Martha wants to have Father committed, but then Martha always did (I think she would like to have the whole family committed, including Berthold).

B insists that the celebrations should proceed as planned, with or without Father. Numerous important people have already indicated their readiness to attend, and relatives, some as far away as the antipodes, have already made their travel arrangements and as far as he is concerned, the day – June 30th – stands.

All the children have phoned to ask how you were and to know if there was anything they could do for you; I said an occasional letter might help.

Patakos and his merry men have shown an unwonted spurt of energy, and he has assured me : 'when missus come home she find new house' (which is what I'm afraid of). All that, however, was last week. Yesterday, possibly hearing that you were better, he arrived bearing a posy of flowers for you ('picked from mine own mother-in-law's garden') and demanded that I pay him the last instalment of his money. I said that he would get it when the job was finished, the mess cleared up and his men had cleared off, which, he said, was exactly what he wanted to do. He was, in fact, all set to have everything finished by the end of the week, but – and here he threw up his hands – his money had run out. He could obtain credit from suppliers but not from his men, and if he couldn't pay them, they wouldn't work. When I reminded him of the terms of our contract he said 'contract is for lawyers' – but his men must eat (his English is improving with his insolence) – I said not another penny, whereupon they all walked off, and I must say it was nice to have the house to myself, even if it was still open to the sky. During the night, however, the skies opened. There was thunder and lightning, wind and rain, and this morning, I am ashamed to say, I gave in. Patakos and his men are now busily back at work, and I have his word of honour that he will finish his job by the end of the week. I hope you will forgive my weakness but I had two considerations. The first is that I would like you to come back to a habitable house. The second is that our ship has finally come in and we would not want to unpack our furniture before the house is ready to receive it.

Things haven't quite worked out the way we had hoped, have they, my dear? – but then things rarely do. My immediate concern is your prompt recovery and I was immensely cheered by your high spirits when I saw you on Sunday. I only hope that you were not putting them on for my benefit. As Stanley used to say, 'Mother's a brick', which of course you are, but I am a fairly mature individual and I hope you aren't hiding anything from me. I am sure that with you restored to your usual vigour, our house restored to us, and our dear old furniture in its place, we should be able to make a new start.

The post here is about as tardy as in England, so the chances are I may be with you before this letter.

All my love,
Your Henry

Dear Stanley,

I am touched by the repeated phone calls. You all seem rather more concerned about me than your mother, and I can't help feeling that you must think that I'm a senile old heap in need of care and attention. I hasten to assure you all, that, though of course I miss your mother, and am concerned about her ill health, I never never felt better and in so far as I need caring at all, I am well, indeed extravagantly, cared for. I may be a good ten years older than your mother, but I have lived a sober life and still have the full use of my faculties. I can get in and out of bed on my own steam, drink a cup of tea without dribbling over my shirt front, and am continent. Moreover, I can open a tin as well as anyone, though so far I have had no cause to.

If I should sound a little aggrieved it is because for all your phone calls you have as yet – neither you, nor William, nor Elaine, nor Helene, nor any of your children – not thought it necessary or proper to put pen to paper to tell us how *you* are. I hate the phone as an instrument (and not only because of its unreliability and expense), but I happen to belong to a generation, to which events only become real when they can be read about. Even your uncle Gerald who, if he ever knew how to write, has probably forgotten, sends the occasional cable and Alice has been in regular correspondence with your mother since we came here.

Having got that off my chest, I can tell you a little more about your mother. She was taken ill in the first place through acute poison administered by a decrepit hack from Jerusalem, and now shows secondary symptoms which have baffled everyone. One doctor says it's a virus, which means he doesn't know; another says it's a streptococcal infection, which presumably means it's a virus. Your mother herself doesn't say anything except to complain at the whole fuss being made about what she calls nothing, but the fact remains that she couldn't keep her food down and was running a very high temperature. They have since contained her temperature, and she is taking food again, albeit in small quantities. She seemed reasonably alright, and if she had shown a little of her acerbity I would have been inclined to believe her. She also showed less than her usual impatience, suffered me to talk for hours on end, and asked me to bring the grandchildren's photos, and I'm afraid I left feeling rather troubled and worried, though I hope I didn't show it. I am seeing her again tomorrow and hope I may be able to give you more cheerful news in the near future.

Your loving father,
Henry

Dear Berthold,

I know you have a heavy cross to bear (two crosses if we include Gwendoline), and it's true I have been rather tardy in answering your letters, but things have not been entirely without incident here. There was first of all Celeste's sudden and dramatic relapse, and now we have had a sudden and equally dramatic recovery. We don't know what brought on her relapse, but I can tell you what brought on the recovery – WRATH.

And there have been secondary events. Yesterday morning I set out to visit Celeste in my newly serviced car. I hadn't gone a hundred yards when a wheel came off. I put the wheel back on but the brakes failed and I abandoned the car by the roadside. Humphry then came to the rescue with a car which he said he had borrowed from a friend. It seemed fairly roadworthy, which is more than I could say of Humphry, but he insisted on driving. We travelled for some distance without mishap, but on the outskirts of Tel Aviv we were stopped by a police car, and Humphry was found to be without a licence, without insurance, without any of the usual documents one needs to do anything round here, and, what is more, without proof that he had the rightful use of the car. It had, apparently, been stolen that morning. 'Stolen?' said Humphry, 'that's the last time I borrow a car from that sonofabitch.' The police retained the car (and Humphry) and, but for my British passport (God Save the Queen) they would have detained me. I continued the journey by taxi (and even that was not without misadventure, for the driver had no idea how to get there).

When I reached the hospital all was consternation, and the elderly German doctor who had been looking after Celeste was tearing his hair. 'Moroccan crazy people I am used to, crazy Russians I am used to, Americans I would not have as patients, but from the English, at least, I expect sanity. This morning she discharged herself without permission. I have nothing more to do with her. I wash my hands.'

'When?'

'Three hours ago, four hours ago, who knows when.'

I rushed back to Bor Shachor, but she was not at home,

and Nicky hadn't seen any sign of her whatever. What to do next, phone the police? I went to the cocktail cabinet to get myself a drink, but Matthew had been there first, and I put on the kettle instead. If anything untoward had happened the telephone presumably would ring. Just then it rang. It was Patakos. He sounded distraught.

'Your wife, please.'

'She isn't here, can I help you?'

'She is crazy.'

She could be difficult, but it occurred to me that that was not the point of his call.

'Why?' I said, 'where is she?'

'Here in my house.'

He gave me his address and I rushed over to his place in a taxi (again not without mishap, for the driver didn't know where it was). He lived in a well-appointed block of flats on the outskirts of town. There was a police car outside and a small crowd had gathered round the entrance. The lift wasn't in working order and I rushed up the stairs as fast as my breath would let me. Patakos lived on the top floor (he would) and he greeted me on the landing with open arms and I was afraid for a moment that he would kiss me.

'Good, good you here. You speak to her, she is crazy.'

Celeste was seated in an easy chair, with three or four policemen and a policewoman around her. She was admiring the view and hardly looked up when I entered.

'Henry,' she said, 'you're a worm!' And I realised at once what had happened. She had received my letter that morning, had been outraged by my pusillanimity in caving in to Patakos, had discharged herself from hospital, and invaded Patakos's own dwelling.

'Have you brought your pyjamas and tooth-brush?'

'No.'

'Well, you should have done. We're stopping here till our house is finished.'

'Speak with her,' pleaded Patakos.

'Are you sure this is legal, dear?'

'What has that got to do with it?'

'Well, you know.'

'All I know is that Patakos has been in illegal occupation of our house, and I am remaining in occupation of his till he has finished the job to my satisfaction, cleared up and cleared out.'

'I am finishing,' pleaded Patakos.

'When you have finished then we can talk. Besides, I am enjoying the view.'

'You want me to cut my throat?'

'Well, yes, if it would help.'

Patakos rushed from the room tearing his hair. A policeman was on the phone to his superior, who arrived on the spot, summed up the situation at a glance, and fled to reappear some time later with his superior, a man senior enough to wear mufti and glasses, and we all settled down to drink coffee.

'I must say Israel policemen are wonderful,' said Celeste.

'You are a very difficult woman,' said the man in mufti. 'Is this how the English behave?'

'Certainly, squatting is an old English custom.'

Later in the day somebody from the Israel Foreign Office appeared in the company of an official from the British Embassy. They too stayed for coffee. In the meantime the crowd outside grew and a television van pulled up with a cameraman on the roof.

We remained in occupation for less than thirty-six hours within which time Patakos augmented his work force and finished the job.

Celeste sent me out to see that everything was in order and complete to my satisfaction before leaving the house, which she did to the applause of the neighbourhood. She had become a celebrity.

When we got back we found Humphry waiting for us (a little shamefacedly, I thought). I wasn't sure if he had been tried and put on probation, or released on bail or simply set free. When I asked what had happened he said simply: 'Is alright.'

Celeste certainly seems none the worse for her ordeal. On the contrary, she looks better than she has been for a long time. She is one of those frail English ladies who are sustained by periodic bursts of fury.

She went with me to the garage to lodge a formal complaint about their so-called servicing of my car. They had seen her on television and dived for cover as soon as she appeared. We eventually cornered the proprietor who not only undertook to put the car right, but as proof of his goodwill allowed me the use of his Peugeot until it was put right.

I am sorry that Gwendoline has had yet another disappointment. One would have thought that at her age she would have given up hope. I always despair when I detect a soft, lyrical tone to her letters, indicating that she has discovered yet another object for her affections, but the denouement is always the same. Where she is willing, they are not and where they are, she thinks they're after her money. Given the state of the family finances, she should be flattered.

What you write about Miss Naysmith is disturbing, but I would not attempt to replace her, not while Father is in his present mood, and his moods, as you know, can last up to five years.

Perhaps Gerald might be induced to come out on a visit, for as you know Father reveres Gerald as the only one of his children to have done anything with themselves, which is to say, he has made a great deal of money. Don't write to him, for he never answers. Phone, and again not to his office, for you'll never get past his personal assistant's secretary's secretary, but to his home, and even if you don't get hold of him there you can always depend on Alice to pass on the message. How a man like him could have married and kept a girl like her is a constant source of wonder to me. She's his saving grace. What did she see in him? It isn't even that she needed his money, and in any case he didn't have it at the time they married. I suppose it is his thrusting, assertive manner. You and I think twice before we clear our throats, which is why he's got where he is, and why we've got where we are. I do not, of course, begrudge him his success, but I probably begrudge him his Alice. It disturbs one's faith in the justice of Providence. One likes to think that a man as successful in business as he is, has an unhappy domestic life, but on the contrary his children are as intelligent and obedient as his wife is beautiful and tender. She is even, which in my experience nice people never are, a good cook. I am not, of course, suggesting that the fates have been unkind to you or me, but I sometimes feel they could have done a little more for Gwendoline. I also used to feel rather sorry for Matthew, but I am no longer so sure that he is the lonely, derelict figure he appears to be. He doesn't say much, and I sometimes get the feeling that people who say little have got something that others haven't, which is why they say little. I sometimes even suspect that he feels sorry for me.

Yours ever,
Henry

Chapter 2

Home Thoughts from Abroad

Dear Gwendoline,

After the various traumas of settling in, settling down and settling up, we are at last beginning to enjoy our stay. We have got rid of the builders (who have done a fairly solid job, though door-handles still keep coming away in the hand), our furniture has arrived and we are at home in our own place in the sun. We have a lovely house, with walls as thick as Windsor Castle, of white limestone, with shaded verandahs fore and aft. The front verandah opens into the main lounge which runs the entire breadth of the house with a bay window looking out on the road, and a French window opening into the garden. Our furniture doesn't quite go with the building, especially the four-poster in the main bedroom (the workmen thought it was a particularly English type of *chupah* which enabled the couple to consummate their marriage the moment they were man and wife) but in any case we can't really afford new furniture, and even if we could we are too used to our old bits and pieces to be parted from them, and when we sit out on the verandah of an evening we keep wondering why we waited till our old age to come out, and why we didn't emigrate once the children were old enough to leave home – or indeed before.

Yet there are moments when I feel like throwing everything up and returning to the chilly mists of England. One such moment – in fact it lasted all day – occurred last week when I went to Ashdod to clear our furniture from the customs.

I had arranged for a large lorry to stand by and, as everything was in one large container, I thought the whole business might not take more than a morning. I should have known better. Gary, whose ship had docked at Haifa, told me he was involved in seven journeys to and from the place before he could retrieve his possessions, but then Gary is the sort of person that that sort of thing happens to. I prided myself with being rather more organised, and I arrived and promptly presented the appropriate papers at the appropriate desk, which in the event turned out to be the inappropriate desk and the clerk sent me to another who dispatched me to a third, who directed me to a fourth, who sent me on to a fifth, but as they were all under the same roof and on the one floor it didn't take too long (though it would have been useful to have had a bicycle). It was when I finally found myself at the sixth desk that an obstacle course presented itself in the person of a short semi-shaven man in thick glasses who was busy finishing off a late breakfast or maybe an early lunch and didn't seem too happy about being disturbed. He examined my passport with a disapproving look.

'Wrong stamp,' he said.

We had arrived as immigrants, and my passport had apparently been stamped as a tourist.

'Look,' I said, 'that's not my fault. We're here to stay, that's our household furniture.'

'What you need household furniture for if you're tourists?'

'We're not tourists, we're here to stay.'

'It says here tourist.'

I asked for his superior.

'Superior?'

'The manager – the *menahel*.'

'I'm the *menahel*.'

'I want the top *menahel*.'

He picked up my papers and shuffled out of the room, to return a few minutes later with a lean man with large glasses.

'You have been here eight months,' he said.

'Yes.'

'Your visa is not renewed.'

'I didn't know I had to renew it – '

'Every tourist must have his passport stamped after three months.'

'We're not tourists.'

'It says here – '

'I don't care what it says there, we're here to stay.'

'To stay?'

'To stay.'

That took him back a bit, and he retired behind a glass partition to speak to someone on the phone, and the *menahel*, with the top *menahel* were joined eventually by the supreme *menahel*, a short man with a large head and a brisk manner. He flicked through my passport, and said : 'There has been a mistake.'

'That's fairly evident, but it's your mistake, not mine.'

'It is simple, all you have to do is to go to Jerusalem – '

'Why should I have to go to Jerusalem, my goods are here?'

'Jerusalem is head office – '

'That's not my concern. I have already spent a day coming here, I shall not spend another going to Jerusalem. Besides, I have a lorry waiting.'

'Aha. I have a better idea, why not pay the duty, and when you have the passport endorsed as an immigrant, you'll get your money back – '

I didn't argue any more but phoned Matthew, who phoned a friend in the British Embassy, who phoned a contact in the Israel Foreign Office, who phoned a friend in the Ministry of the Interior, who phoned the head of customs and excise in Ashdod. By then, however, it was lunch or tea or half-day or something and the port closed, and when the port is closed nothing short of total war can open it. I eventually retrieved my goods without entirely losing my sanity, two days later.

We've also had some difficulty with our health insurance. There is something called the Kupat Cholim, which is roughly akin to our Health Service, whose doctors are fairly proficient, but one can expire while waiting to see them. We tried a commercial medical insurance group, whose premiums are fairly reasonable but which cover one for every contingency short of ill health, so for small complaints we depend on the advice of our local chemist (who generally sends us home with a kind of stomach powder), and for large we pay through the nose.

We've had to change our eating habits for many of my favourite foods are unobtainable here, or obtainable at a price which would make me lose my appetite, so it's goodbye to kippers and rice krispies, but the more exotic vegetables like avocados and peppers, which are expensive in London are fairly reasonable here. Butter is a luxury and is sold in neat little packs like two-ounce chocolate bars.

Our American neighbours have urged us to get a deep freeze and to stock up once a week or even once a month, but Celeste feels too old to adapt herself to such contraptions, besides which we enjoy our daily shopping trips into town. Most of the shops, including the local supermarket, are grouped round three sides of a fairly spacious piazza. The buildings are neither handsome nor gracious and remind one at first glance of one of those forts in the old French Foreign Legion films, but the whole place has a certain gaiety, especially after five in the afternoon when the worst heat of the day is over, a breeze begins to ruffle the trees, and people come out to take the air, do their shopping, sit in the cafés to see and be seen. The open side of the piazza looks out on a small park, with an avenue of lofty date palms shading a coarse lawn with hissing sprinklers, and a large kiosk which seems to be the main hub of the area. One gets the impression that half of the town lives on feeding the other half, for cafés seem to alternate with pizza parlours, wimpy bars and restaurants, some a little grubby, others well appointed and clean, and the cafés extend their chairs onto the pavement, boulevard style.

Most people seem to eat out (not in restaurants which is but an expensive way of eating in), but right out in the street, and if you encounter someone who is not talking he, or more usually she, is munching pizza, falafal, corn on the cob (held between two hands and played back and forward like a mouth-organ), Danish pastries, hot-dogs, cold-dogs, wimpys, ice-cream. Cheeks bulge and jaws grind, and all with an earnestness as if every bite taken will be the last. The habit is catching and I have been known to lick an ice-cream in public myself. Celeste says I'm turning native.

Celeste and I tend to prefer town in the morning, when it is somewhat quieter and less crowded. Everybody seems to be at work here and when we come in from our shopping about eleven, the only people we encounter are ancients like ourselves, or raucous young mums with raucous young children (when I say it is *quieter* in the morning I do not mean that it is ever quiet. That it never is, and if one should come upon an hour of the night when people are silent, the cats – which are as scraggy, half wild and as verminous as in Venice – take over). We have discovered a café called Kapulskis with the most delicious pastries which remind me of those heavenly cream puffs we had that summer in Bad Ischel when Father took us to the Salzkammergut. Remember them? Nectar trapped in cream! The coffee is also good and we like to sit out under the awning and enjoy a slow cup. We are there every day and indeed have become one of the sights of the town, and when an occasional bus-load of tourists is discharged into the piazza, I have an uncomfortable feeling that we are pointed out as such by the guide.

I am known in town as *ha-kovah*, the hat, a nomenclature acquired after my first visit to synagogue. I arrived, as I always do in such a place, in my bowler, which occasioned disapproving glances on every side. They obviously thought it was some sort of fancy crash-helmet, and at the end of the service the Rabbi took me aside to suggest that it was perhaps inappropriate gear for a house of worship, to which I pointed out that it was the hat traditionally worn by Jews in England, and certainly by the menfolk in our family, when attending service, and it was a tradition to which I meant to adhere.

'Ah,' he said, 'ah, tradition is good. Is Holy. You should have said so.'

'I am saying so.'

'All Jews wear this?'

'Not all.'

'Is very nice.'

To cut a long story short he left me his size and I promised to get him a bowler when I was next in London.

It gets hot in the afternoon and I generally (invariably) sleep, but Celeste, mad dog that she is, is out in the midday sun, though what she can find to do with herself at such a time, I daren't ask.

We have found a Romanian restaurant which has a fairly good pseudo-French cuisine, but as soon as we appeared the proprietor rushed into his kitchen and ordered 'a special' for us. 'I know what Englishman like,' he said, with a self-satisfied chuckle, and in due course he presented us with fish and chips, but as the fish was red mullet and the chips and the fish were fried in olive oil, we could hardly complain. There is also a local white wine with a slightly acrid flavour, not unlike a good Riesling, which costs about ten shillings a bottle and which I take in fairly copious quantities. Celeste says it will ruin my liver, but my innards have had a fairly sheltered existence and it may be salutary to expose them to the occasional hazard.

We have made quite a number of friends, apart from the Gittlesons whom I have mentioned before. We are often joined at coffee on the piazza by a Mr Nahumi who owns a 'large' textile factory (no one round here confesses to anything small), but whatever the nature of his responsibility it leaves him ample time to drink innumerable cups of coffee with whole slabs of Apfelstrudel. He is, unlike anyone we have met so far, a relaxed, amiable, egg-shaped man (incidentally, if you think all fat men sleep o'nights, I can introduce you to a few round here who don't) who seems to know something about everything, or at least enough to talk endlessly about almost every subject under the sun.

He came from Germany about forty years ago without a penny in his pocket (though he doesn't look as if his pockets are overloaded even now) and changed his name to Nahumi (from something I can't pronounce and will not attempt to spell). He is apparently from a well-known German-Jewish family, but once he set foot in Palestine he decided to leave his German past completely behind him, though his Cherman accent is still very much with him, or perhaps one imagines it, for he looks and behaves as if he should have a Cherman accent very much as Matthew looks as if he should have a pukka English accent (which, of course, he does).

When I told him my name he asked if we were related

to the Hochs of Klagenfurt and, if so, he believes that his
father did business with ours. As Father has done business with
almost everybody, there is a mathematical probability that he
did.

I have been toying vaguely with the idea of Hebraising my
name. You were too young to remember, but Hoch was a
troublesome name to have during World War I and people
thought we were Germans, and even when Berthold and
Matthew were called to the colours and were wearing the
King's uniform they had to go around explaining that they
were not, and never had been, German, and I suppose we
stuck to the name because it would have been rather *arriviste*
to change it. It didn't, of course, prevent Gerald from changing his name to Higham as soon as he took out American
citizenship, but then, of course, he is a *parvenu*. Nahumi's
case for name-changing is that it makes you feel at one with
the place. The Hebrew equivalent of Hoch is Rom or Govoha
or Givati, but none of them sound right. I could, I suppose,
adopt Father's first name and call myself Ben Shlomo, but
that doesn't sound right either, besides which there is something to be said for holding on to all the intrinsic elements
of oneself, including one's name, and really I do like the sound
of Hoch, it has a thrust to it.

Nor would it, I think, be immodest to claim that the name
Hoch stands for something in England, and I hope that
neither Celeste nor I are too old to make it count for something in Israel.

You ask me if there is anything we miss about England.
Four things off-hand, the Fox and Hounds, liquorice allsorts,
and television and tea-time. We don't watch much television
here, but we hear a great deal of it, mostly against our will,
especially in the hot weather when viewers sit out on their
balconies and have their sets blare at them from the depths of
their living rooms. There was a power cut the other night and
it was paradise. Celeste and I dined out on the verandah, by
candle-light. There were still transistors crackling about us in
the darkness, but they sounded like crickets. 'I wish we could
have power cuts every night,' said Celeste, at which Humphry, who happened to be nearby, said : 'I fix it.'

We still, of course, have tea at tea-time here, but nobody else does, partly because there is no closed season for snacks and beverages in this country, people eat and drink round the clock, and even where they do have tea it's always by the glass. I have never seen a tea-pot, cosy, a cake-stand or any of the other paraphernalia of tea-time since we left London. Moreover, a ritual isn't quite a ritual if celebrated in isolation, even though we now have the use of our own silverware and china. When we sat down for our tea about four or five in the afternoon in Isleworth, one was conscious of the clink of cup on saucer in a million homes, the stirring of sugar, the crunch of teeth on toast. A sense of tranquillity descended with the first sip and I suppose it was less of a meal than a form of meditation. One felt it to be, especially if the curtains were drawn against the torrent of traffic outside, the calmest time of day.

Here tea-time is the most boisterous time of day. The place comes alive and shrill voices rent the air, and when Celeste and I sit down to our tea and toast and cake (local pastries, as I said, are excellent, but we do miss Fuller's walnut cake) we feel strongly removed from the world about us.

Matthew sends his love. He is still with us but spends most of his time with the Gittlesons and comes here only to sleep (and sometimes, I suspect, not even that). He appears to have made an immense impression on Gary (Mr Gittleson), mainly, I suspect, because Gary, like so many Americans, is an incurable Anglophile. I don't know why he should be, because he hardly knows England (perhaps that's why he is) and Matthew is, so to speak, a bit of olde England on the hoof. It was Celeste who, if you remember, once said that he reminds her of a horse-hair sofa. I didn't quite see what she meant then, but I do now.

On warm evenings he holds court on the Gittleson's balcony, with Gary and Nicky and their two sons sitting in silence round his feet, while he crackles on about his days in India and Ceylon, and the Turks and Caicos Islands, pausing only for a sip of brandy, or to permit Gary to re-charge his cup. I have never known him to be so prolix, but then he has never had such an eager audience.

Sometimes Gary might interrupt and ask in an awed voice why he was sent to one outpost rather than another.

'Don't suppose they knew what to do with me,' he would say, 'not that I had much to do. I was the odd dog's-body. Stamped passports, kept down mosquitoes, that sort of thing' – all of which makes him sound very modest, though, of course, he was nothing but a dog's-body in those early days. He does have quite a gift for passing off a plain statement of fact as an understatement.

He also talks about his boyhood in Fetlock Hall and without uttering an untrue word or even an exaggeration leaves his hearers with the impression that it is an Elizabethan mansion on the scale of, say, Hatfield House, especially when he talks about the butler, and the servants and the tenants and the 'game-keeper'. (Old George did call himself a game-keeper, but was he not employed on the estate mainly to keep down the rats?)

'Did you have a ghost?' Nicky asked him once.

'You mean a headless nun, that sort of thing?'

'Yes.'

'I should imagine not.' – The sort of no which hearers often take to mean yes, and I sometimes ask myself if our brother Matthew is not perhaps something of a charlatan. I should imagine not.

Your loving brother,
Henry

Dear Berthold,

I think I shall have to foreswear the pleasure of writing to Gwendoline.

I sent her a bright letter full of chat and pleasantries to cheer her up, and she retorts with a bill of grievances, which I sum up under the following headings:

1. That I regard her 'with despair as someone whom life has passed by'. To be sure I regard her with despair (who does not?) but if life has passed her by it is at least partly because she has kept it at arm's length.

2. That if I have anything of import I write it to you, and

that I fob her off with trivialities and chit-chat. So much for my attempts to cheer her up.

3. That Celeste had been 'on the point of death', and I hadn't told her. I did in fact write that Celeste was ill, and as for her being 'on the point of death', that, said Celeste, was wishful thinking.

4. That I am selfish and self-indulgent, that I was not interested in her problems, and that I had only settled in Israel because I wanted to run away from my responsibilities. I have not looked at it like that, but she may be right. On the other hand it would, I suppose, be futile to point out the number of occasions when I have tried to be of help, and when my efforts have been not only abortive but misconstrued.

5. That I overlooked her birthday, which is true, but I did so out of charity. I seem to recall that last year when I *did* remember her birthday, she accused me of trying to humiliate her.

6. That Celeste and I are determined not to have her set foot over my threshold. It is true that I advised her not to come until our house was complete. It is further true that our house is now complete but in fact we did invite her to come, to which she complains that I did so in general terms, and that an invitation to be sincere must be specific. But when am I to invite her? It is now May. In another six weeks we shall be in England and I suggested that she might want to come back with us, to which she replied that it would be August by then, and that I knew very well that she went up to the Edinburgh Festival every August. I didn't, did you? For all I knew she could have been away grouse shooting.

If she can upset me in this way at this distance, I can imagine what it must be like having her under the same roof. Martha, no doubt, would like to have her committed, and who can blame her, but can I suggest something less drastic? I do so with some hesitation, for she has already had innumerable disappointments and I would not wish to add to them, but an acquaintance from Bor Shachor will be in London shortly and I suggested that he looked you (i.e. Gwendoline) up. He is a Mr Nahumi, whom I may have mentioned to you before, and who believes he may have met you, or at least

Father, before the war, though of course Hoch is such a common name that he is not too sure. He is a man of substance, in more ways than one, respectable, respected and one of the foremost citizens of the town, indeed one of its founding fathers. He may be a year or two younger or older than Gwendoline, which is to say he is – as she is – of a vintage where age differences blur. He is no Adonis, but on the other hand he is a relaxed, amiable man, even if his expression is a little forbidding. He is a widower, and I have the impression that he would like to remarry, if only because he cannot keep house alone and has had unfortunate experiences with his housekeepers (to which you may ask, who hasn't?).

He has some business in London shortly and will be staying at the Kenilworth Hotel, Bloomsbury (which may suggest that he is of modest means, but in fact he is only a modest spender), and I've asked him to call you. I appreciate it would be awkward to have him with you at this moment on top of everything else but he could be the answer to all our prayers. I must confess that I gave him your telephone number with some hesitation and I have been asking myself what has he done to me that I should wish to inflict Gwendoline upon him, but of course it's one thing to have a woman as a sister and quite another as a wife, and people do change. Nahumi has two grown-up sons who look after his business and indeed look after it so well that they have more or less thrown him out of it – now there's a familiar tale – but he's as well off as anyone in Israel can be without actually stealing, which does not, however, mean that he could keep Gwendoline in the manner to which she's been accustomed. I doubt if anyone can these days. Father over-indulged her, which I believe, is at the source of her trouble, and you, if you don't mind my saying so, seem to be doing the same.

Nahumi showed me a photo of his late wife. She had the great height and the formidable profile of our dear sister, though not, I gather, her formidable temper. It would be nice if something came of it, but that of course will not solve your immediate problem and I can well imagine that having her and Father on your hands at the same time, plus the centenary celebrations, may be too much and I wonder if we can't cancel them. It would be a great pity, of course, and we are all looking forward to them, but there is no point in killing yourself to arrange a programme of festivities which Father says he does not want, and which, between ourselves, he doesn't deserve. Or have arrangements been carried too far for that?

We (including, alas, Matthew) have booked to fly out on June 28th, and we would in normal circumstances have been able to put forward our journey by several weeks, but circumstances here are rarely normal. Our garage roof caved in the other night and virtually demolished the car and we had to evacuate the house (and move in with the Gittlesons) in case it should have the same structural defects. We have been assured it is safe, but even so we no longer feel secure under our own roof, and I instinctively reach out for my old Home Guard helmet every time I hear the slightest noise. No doubt we will get over it. In the meantime we have briefed a lawyer and are suing Patakos both for garage and car. (He is lucky not to face a charge of manslaughter, for, had the roof caved in a moment earlier, it would have demolished Celeste as well.)

He is, he said, reserving his defence but, reservations apart, he pointed out that the garage had been sub-contracted, that he was away on reserve duty while it was being built, that his father had died, that we had asked for a cheap job and had got one, and in any case who in Israel needs a garage? Moreover, he had fought in the War of Independence and had been wounded in the head. To which Celeste retorted that I had fought in the First World War and had been gassed in the trenches, and that I had been in the Home Guard in the second. 'Ah,' he said, 'but has he been shot in the head?'

Patakos, in other words, is not an easy man to argue with and we are leaving the matter to the lawyers, but in the meantime we would find it difficult to leave home.

I've told Matthew about your troubles and he has offered to fly out earlier, but I am not convinced that he would alleviate them and might well add to them.

You seem to be nervous of approaching Gerald at all. I suppose we are all in such awe of his success that we are afraid to ask him for anything, but he is Father's son, the same as we are, and should be reminded of his responsibilities. If you don't want to approach him, I shall.

Yours ever,
Henry

Dear Gerald,

Crisis! Father is himself, Gwendoline is herself, and Berthold is beside himself. And Miss Naysmith, who used to be of help at such times, has become a problem in her own right. She tried to stifle Father the other night as if he was Desdemona and although she protested that she was doing it all for his own good and the good of the family, Berthold no longer feels he can leave her in charge and is more or less a prisoner of the Hall. Martha wants to have both Father and Miss Naysmith committed. Half the servants have given notice to leave, the other half have left without notice, and the central heating, which is kept on all the year round for the sake of Father, has broken down. What is more to the point I fear the imminent breakdown of Berthold, and with him out of the way, there is every possibility that Miss Naysmith could run amok, and massacre the whole household – which, you will remember, she frequently threatened to do when we were young, and she has now reached the pitch when one must take her at her word.

I hope I do not sound alarmist, but that in fact is the situation, and unless you or I fly out without delay the centenary celebrations to which you and I have been looking forward so eagerly may turn into a wake. Unhappily I am not in a position to leave Israel at the moment for reasons which I shall explain later. In any case I find I am generally of little help in such a situation as I tend to get in people's way, and even where I don't, Father has never had much patience with me. I am not really sure why. I was never a troublesome child and, but for bouts of ill health, not too awkward an adult, yet he treats me as if I was a congenital idiot. Certainly he almost never addresses me without raising his voice, and I have often asked myself if he thinks I'm deaf. You, on the other hand, have always been his favourite. You're the youngest, you had the good sense to leave home early and, above all, you never went into the company. You have launched out on your own and have become a Hoch in your own right, as successful as Father, perhaps even more so, and he looks at you and sees himself. I suppose it's a form of narcissism, but you are his idol. He was of course proud of Matthew for many years, especially when he got his CBE, but a gong is no substitute for a daughter-in-law and grandchildren and Matthew has failed in his primary duty of contributing his share to the future supply of Hochs. Father often boasts of the start he gave us in life, but he has never quite forgiven Berthold and me for making use of it. I'm a little sorry now that we did. Berthold certainly could have prospered without him and only went into the company – and is staying in it – out of a sense of duty, and now, of course, the poor chap has everything on top of him, with everything and everyone, but especially Father, at their most impossible. Could you and/or Alice not bring forward your trip by a week or two? I know you're busy if only because of the infrequency with which you answer my letters (I do not consider the cables you dart off in lieu of letters an adequate reply). You have presumably made your first billion, and I am told that once you have done that, the second billion can be left to make itself. In any case could you contact B right away by letter or phone? Do NOT telex or cable. Cables in England still mean bad news.

To turn to another topic. Do you remember expressing an interest in that large Moorish villa near ours? If you are still interested I would urge you to put in a bid now, for there is something a-stirring behind its high walls and we have heard rumours that it might be taken over for some sort of youth club. We have been here nine months now and have inured ourselves to everything except the young. You and I (or at least Berthold and I) were brought up to believe that children should be seen but not heard, and if they weren't seen either that was better still. Here they are brought up to believe that the young shall inherit the earth and they act as if they have already done so. Everything is built round them and for them, and there is no more startling sight for a man of my generation than to be confronted suddenly with a school disgorging its young. It's like a river bursting its banks, hurtling torrents in all directions, shouting, pushing, jostling, overflowing from the pavements into the roads and from the roads into the shops. I was once caught in such a flood. Had I been a younger man I would have run; as it was I stood rooted to the spot and let the tide swirl about me. I emerged unscathed in body, but was rather shaken in spirit.

If any number of them are to form a colony next door, we shall have to move from our house beautiful, but to where I know not.

Celeste is making urgent inquiries to see if there is any truth in the rumour, not that we could do anything about it if there were. If they were planning to take the house over for an old-age home, or a lunatic asylum or a leper colony, one could raise objections and be sure of a hearing, but one only has to utter the word 'youth' in this country and all argument stops. For all I know the same is true of England, but we remained unaware of it in our cosy corner of Isleworth. Make one change and you suddenly become aware of all the others.

Americans, and especially American children, are supposed to be noisy, but we have an American family next door with two children as silent as mice except, that is, when they are practising an instrument, which they do at all times of the day and most times of the night. The mother is a fairly accomplished flautist, the father plays the piano and the children are encumbered with various stringed instruments and also play woodwind. The father, who has the disposition of a recluse and who seems to shun his own shadow, was, believe it or not, in advertising. He has struck up an improbable friendship with our brother, the ex-pro-consul, and has as a result become a student and admirer of the British Empire and has even suggested that the source of all American misfortunes goes back to the rebellion against George III.

All of which brings me back to England, Father and Berthold. Can I rely on you to phone him, for apart from his troubles at home, he has had continuous business worries? I don't know why he should have them because his children relieved him of his responsibilities almost as soon as he passed over his shares, and his position of Chairman is hardly more than a sinecure (though a highly paid one). He still goes into the office several times a week (or at least he did before Miss Naysmith went berserk), but that was mainly at Martha's bidding, and as far as I understand all that he does with himself is to shuffle around his own private share portfolio, which is perhaps why he's so worried. All in all this is not an easy time for anyone trying to make an honest or, for that matter, a dishonest penny in England.

I am glad that I retired when I did, though, of course, what I retired on is declining in value day by day. Celeste said to me the other day when I wanted to splash out on something: 'You daren't, Henry, you must face the fact that your family suffers from chronic longevity.' The way she put it made it sound like haemophilia. Still the boys are doing alright (given the tastes and habits of their wives, they have to). The only shadow over my life (apart from Gwendoline, of course) is young Rodney, who keeps making reverse-charge calls from various corners of the globe to tell us nothing in particular. I wouldn't even mind if he was doing nothing, provided he kept doing it in the same place.

Love to Alice and the children,

Yours,
Henry

Dear William,

You seem rather upset that I wrote to Stanley but didn't write to you, but I was feeling rather depressed at the time and discharged my heartache at the first name which came to mind. Besides which I gathered that you were about to embark for the West Indies. Let me hasten to assure you that your mother is now restored to perfect health, the best proof of which is that she is becoming restless, and is talking about finding a job, or a cause, possibly both, though at this moment she is on a shopping spree in Tel Aviv to find presents for the various grandchildren and, of course, for Father. What does one get for a strong-willed centenarian with pronounced individual taste, who has everything but who has outlived most of his faculties? Helene is good at that sort of thing. Any ideas?

We were charmed by the letters from the children, and especially Julie's portrait of you and Helene. It may not be a particularly flattering portrait (at least not of Helene) but it is very well done and I intend to have it framed. She is obviously a very gifted child and the talent I suppose must come from Helene. We have various talents in our side of the family, commercial (Father and Gerald, perhaps even Berthold), gubernatorial (Matthew), legal (you and Stanley), but none of us have shown any inclination to the arts. Rodney, it is true, does write a little, but I wish he wouldn't for he sends us clippings of his work from time to time from journals I'd never heard of before and wouldn't care to hear of again, on the way schools are used to keep the poor in ignorance and subjects of that ilk, and in so far as I can make sense of them at all, they are quite mad. I know that you and, to a lesser extent, Stanley tend to be rather dismissive about Rodney and I suppose one does have to be a father to have much patience for such a son, but it does seem to me that a young man who can make plain common sense stand on its head, does show a certain mental agility. Father, as you may know, was originally intended for the Rabbinate and he used to tell us how, as a young man in Yeshiva, he was trained to demonstrate not only that black is black and that white is black, but that there is no contradiction between the two propositions. Perhaps Rodney should be a Rabbi. I know that it is difficult nowadays to bring young men round to a belief in God, but he believes in so many impossible things that he should be able to take God in his stride. I shall speak to him about it when I'm in London next month, and perhaps I may have a word with the Chief Rabbi.

I need hardly add that we are both looking forward to seeing you all very much.

My love to Helene and the children,

Your loving father,
Henry

Dear Berthold,

I was immensely cheered both by the tone and contents of your letter. Alice was obviously the cure Father needed, and as you say, he finds qualities in his daughters-in-law which he does not always see in his children. If you will remember, he always wanted a daughter, and rather expected me to be one and I feel that he hasn't quite forgiven me for being something else, and Gwendoline, when she finally did materialise, was such an awkward and unlovely infant that, as he once remarked, 'she might as well have been a boy', and I think the reason why he passed over the major part of his fortune to her was that he wanted to redress an injustice of nature. Alice may, as you say, be his favourite daughter-in-law because she happens to be the wife of his favourite son, but I think I would not be doing an injustice to your dear wife or mine, to suggest that she does have something special, and that she continues to keep it even though she is now in her fifties (American women never do seem to show their age – it's the men who put on the years on their behalf, rather like the picture of Dorian Gray). And it does say something for Father that he is, even at his great age, still alive to her charms.

Are you quite sure you'll be able to put us all up at Fetlock Hall? Don't forget there'll be four people in Gerald's party and three in mine (including Matthew). I presume we will not be the only guests in residence. Would it not be better to book us in at the Fox and Hounds? I have happy memories of the place and it would not be too expensive. (Matthew, by the way, also wants to be booked in at the Fox and Hounds, but that would not be a good idea at all.)

We are at a loss on what to get Father. You may remember last year, when I bought him a leather-bound album with photos of our children and grandchildren, he threw it at me. Does he still save stamps? Celeste suggested that we get him a complete set of Israeli stamps from Independence to date.

I also feel the need to bring a little something to Gwendoline, but there's always the risk that whatever I bring might prove offensive, though presumably not as offensive as bringing nothing at all, which is what I'm tempted to do. Celeste has suggested an illustrated edition of the *Song of Songs*, but it is so full of phrases that can be given so many different meanings that I fear she may mis-read it.

Celeste herself, by the way, reads all such matter in the original now. I must say I marvel at my dear wife. We have been here for under a year and do you know that she is almost proficient in Hebrew? We used to attend something called an *Ulpan* every morning where they teach newcomers the language. We were a motley pack consisting of a pair of silent, hydrocephalic men with dusky skins and large eyes, who came from a remote corner of the Caucasus and spoke some obscure dialect unknown to anyone in Israel, and who never batted an eyelid nor uttered a word and who may, for all I know, have been deaf and dumb; three or four voluble stout parties from Muscovy proper; an intense-looking young man from Kiev, who was the swot of the class and graduated from it after about a month; Gary Gittleson, who was very conscientious but not very bright; a Cockney pair from East London, whose English was totally unintelligible to our teacher and for whom Celeste acted as interpreter; a Sef Efrican whose English was unintelligible even to Celeste (perhaps he speaks Afrikaans); a swaggering little Argentinian in a black beret and with a Cesar Romero moustache; two or three cheerful Romanians with gold teeth who seemed to be in class to do business rather than learn Hebrew and who waylaid all newcomers from hard-currency countries (it says something about the strength of sterling that they leave Celeste and me severely alone); and a pair of pedantic Frenchwomen, maiden ladies, who hadn't been in the class a week before they started putting the teacher right. I used to be rather good at Hebrew when I was a boy, but all my knowledge seems to have deserted me. Moreover, Hebrew is full of similar-sounding words which have radically different meanings and I cause the most outrageous howlers, not a few of them obscene, every time I open my mouth, and my written work is such that our teacher, a chaste, Orthodox matron with a kerchiefed head, is rather nervous of handling it. To give but one example the word *zemira*, meaning song, when slightly misspelt, reads *zemorah*, meaning penis, and I once came out with the splendid sentence : 'His penis caught the ear of his beloved.' My memory is also not what it was and after three or four months of torment I have had to drop out. Celeste, on the other hand, has been the prize pupil. Moreover, she became a shop-steward and when they raised the fees abruptly, she led the delegation of protest and had them reduced, and when our teacher had to retire because of a premature birth (brought on, they say, by one of my essays), it was Celeste who presented her with a gift on behalf of the class.

We had our first outing to the pictures a few weeks ago. It was a Swedish film dubbed in American with Hebrew and Arabic sub-titles. We did not see very much of it because from time to time the film jammed in and at other times it was shown backwards or upside down, which, for all I know, may have been an improvement for if one does have to watch couples fornicating, there is something to be said for seeing them doing it on their heads. What was intolerable was the rowdiness, people chattering at the tops of their voices, or shouting across the stalls to friends in other parts of the building, or clattering back and forward to buy food in the vestibule, or guzzling pop, or rolling empty bottles down the floor, or making suggestive noises, or shouting ribald comments on the events on screen. There were attendants around the place, but the only time they intervened was to save a young girl from what appeared to be rape. Celeste tried to silence some yobs beside us by glaring at them, which is difficult in the dark, and she ended by threatening them with her handbag, which was more effective, but only in the immediate vicinity, and after suffering this for about half an hour, we walked out and demanded to see the *menahel* – the manager. The attendant, needless to say, claimed to be the manager, so we asked for the chief *menahel*, and were eventually led to the projection room where a stout man in glasses was struggling to extricate a film from the machine, and we left the protests till the following morning.

The manager was unapologetic. His projectionist, he said, was in the army, so he had to do everything himself; as for the crowds, he admitted they were rowdy, but he was glad they were there at all. Television was killing the trade and it was such a struggle to keep his head above water, that he sometimes wished he had his head in the ground.

Celeste suggested that if he showed more wholesome fare he might get a more wholesome audience.

'I give people what they want,' he said. 'They want Kung-Fu, I show Kung-Fu, they want Fu-King, I show Fu-King.'

The Gittlesons told us they had given up the cinema after somebody had tried to undo Nicky's jeans. 'It would have been one thing if I'd been there on my own,' she said, 'but Gary was sitting there beside me.' He was really upset and when he protested to the manager he was told: 'So somebody make a mistake, they think she's your sister.' Nahumi said that cinemas were no longer places of entertainment – it's where youngsters go to let off steam if that is the right word for it, in the dark. 'But I like the pictures,' said Celeste, 'they're my favourite form of entertainment.' 'And mine,' said Nicky, and out of that conversation there was born the Bor Shachor Film Club, of which Celeste – need I add? – is chairman. They hire a local cinema and rent their own film and last night they had their opening programme – *Kind Hearts and Coronets*, with Alec Guinness. It was a sell-out and people came from as far afield as Tel Aviv and Ashekelon to see it, but more important it was a get-together for the *pnei ho-ir*, the 'faces of the town', which is to say, 'the people of quality', doctors, dentists, pharmacists, school-masters, local government officials, city councillors, the more substantial burghers, people with jackets to match their trousers, and even ties. And while the company assembled in the foyer, wisps of German and Hungarian intermingled with Russian, English and Hebrew, and there was kissing of hands and, methought, even clicking of heels. After the show people crowded round Celeste to shake her hand and congratulate her, as if she had made the film or starred in it, and for a moment I feared that we might be overtaken by a torrent of speeches, without which no occasion in this country is complete. One gets the feeling that people carry around little prepared texts on their person, much as an Englishman might carry his season ticket, in case they should feel called upon to say 'a few words'. The expression 'a few words' is the only instance of Jewish understatement that I've come across.

Everybody praised Celeste's choice of film and as one

patron observed : 'Ze English sense of humour, she makes me laugh. We need her here.' Apart from the film she had also introduced nice little touches, like having the place swept and cleaned. We had our own honorary stewards, but there was no rowdyism, no rape and no empty fizz bottles. Children were only allowed in (at half price) if accompanied by adults, and no one was allowed to bring food (I don't mean sweets, but in Israel people sometimes bring their supper into the cinema) or drink into the building. Our next film is *Passport to Pimlico*, and we are to have a retrospective season of Greer Garson films, beginning with *Mrs Miniver*.

The case of Us v. Patakos is getting nowhere. I asked Nahumi to recommend a lawyer and he introduced us to an intense-looking young man with glasses, called Michaeli, who turned out to be his son-in-law, and as soon as I mentioned Patakos he threw up his hands.

'Everybody is suing Patakos and everybody is afraid to take him to court, because if he goes to jail his business collapses and if his business collapses no one gets a cent. I suggest we settle out of court.'

'Which means that everyone with money is at the mercy of every pauper.'

'Sure, it is like this everywhere.'

He might have added that the solvent are also at the mercy of their lawyers. Before he took on the case I had to pay him an advance of a hundred pounds (sterling) – which I believe is standard practice round here, though it smacks of sharp practice to me – and hardly was the money paid over than he was called up on reserve duty, and we are left without a lawyer, without a garage, without compensation and without a car.

In the meantime we are making do with taxis and buses. Taxis are cheaper than in England, but the drivers seem unfamiliar with any address beyond their own and the first thing they will ask you when you give them a destination, is : 'Where is it ?' and the second is : 'How do you get there ?'

The buses are inexpensive and frequent and fast, and a journey brings back memories of one's first ride on a switchback. They hurtle along at about seventy miles an hour, with the driver chatting over his shoulder to a chum, one hand on the wheel, the other collecting fares and giving out change, or punching tickets. All the buses have radios which are switched on for the news bulletins, and some blare all the time, usually with pop music, and when I asked one driver if he wouldn't mind turning his radio down, or, preferably off, he asked me how long I had been in the country. 'Nine months,' I said.

'Nine months and you're already telling me what to do with my own bus?'

All the bus companies are co-operatively owned by their drivers and no one will ever know the true meaning of incivility till he has travelled in an Israeli bus and had an exchange with an Israeli bus-driver. In a sense we made a wrong start by using our own car from the day we arrived, for the buses and drivers are an essential part of local lore and one doesn't really know Israel till one has acquired knowledge of both. They get you there and, as often as not, they get you back, but with grudging reluctance, and they are not so much a public service as a public nuisance, though it may be fairly said that anyone who has become a seasoned bus traveller can face the other hardships of life with equanimity, and in that sense it's a useful training. The seats are spaced on the supposition that the country is peopled by compressible midgets with telescopic legs. Floors are unswept, windows are grimy, which is perhaps just as well for they blind one to the hazards of the road, the main hazard being other drivers in other buses. No one gives way until the last moment, and sometimes not even then, and one can rarely go on a longish journey without finding a bus in the ditch with its wheels still turning in the air. Drivers are more inclined to brake than decelerate. Stops are as sudden as starts, and one tumbles along like clothes in a dryer, now thrown forward, now backward and always landing in a heap, and any pregnant woman anxious to be rid of her foetus need only take a ride in a bus. The number twelve from Bor Shachor, which goes along a route with many sharp turns is known as the abortion special. On the longer journeys one benefits from the chumminess induced by shared ordeals and I have made more acquaintances since we've become carless than in all the months before, but if

Israel should ever make peace with the Arabs, the population will turn as one upon its bus-drivers and hang them from their garage rafters.

Is Rodney with you? He said that he was making his way back to England – without saying where from – to attend Father's celebrations when I last spoke to him and it is a week or two since we've heard anything more. We are expecting Gerald here shortly – he is stopping off en route to England.

Finally, to the matter of Nahumi. You asked me about his religion, which is an odd question. He is Jewish, of course, but I should perhaps add of the Reform persuasion. I should not, however, imagine he would object to marrying at an Orthodox ceremony, performed by an Orthodox Rabbi (especially, as is the case with all the marriages in our family, if the Rabbi also happened to be Chief Rabbi). I know that our family have traditionally been pillars of the Orthodox synagogue and that Gwendoline in particular, as with most Jewish womenfolk, is the conscience of the family and is a devout Jewess who insists on kosher food even when eating out, but it's not my impression that she goes to synagogue more than five or six times a year, whereas Nahumi goes every week. (There isn't a Reform synagogue here. They meet in private houses, usually Gary's – Gary in fact is almost the lay Rabbi of the congregation.) Of course, if he was serious about his Reform beliefs that would have been a serious obstacle, but he says he is not by habit a synagogue man and goes mainly because Reform Jews in Israel are a persecuted minority and he likes to give them moral support and indeed Celeste, who is anything but Reformist, has made the same point, and sometimes joins them for prayer on a Friday night. (The matter got to the ear of Rabbi Mittwoch – as everything does – and he put it to her that a woman of her standing should not be seen in such company.)

No, I don't anticipate any difficulties on the matter of religion. Where I do have some trepidation is on the matter of appearances and I think Gwendoline should be warned that Nahumi, though a man of means, verges on the inelegant. He says he hates tailors and fittings and that he can get used to anything except new clothes, and everything about his appearance testifies to this fact. It is not that he is grubby or covered in soup stains and ash. On the contrary, his clothes are spotless, but they were obviously made when he was a much younger and certainly a much slimmer man. His jackets are under great strain and there is always a considerable disengagement area between his trousers and shoes. He also wears a straw hat with the fore-brim turned up à la Bud Flanagan. We are on close terms, but not so close that I can pull him aside and suggest that he gets himself a decent outfit while in London. Bor Shachor is not a place where sartorial solecisms cause eyebrows to be raised and it may be that when abroad he dresses more tastefully. On the other hand one cannot be sure. I would not have thought this a point worth mentioning but for the fact that Gwendoline places great store by appearances, though I am not sure that her own addiction to flappers' weeds would place her amongst the ten best-dressed women in Europe. He should be in London by the time you get this and I do hope that you'll find time to contact him.

Yours ever,
Henry

Dearest Gwendoline,

How was I to know that you had met Nahumi over forty years ago and that you didn't care for him even then – and that even if you had cared for him you would never have married someone with a name like Poetzhaendler? He did tell me what his name had been, but it didn't sound like Poetzhaendler (how does one pronounce it in any case?). And isn't what his name *was* a little beside the point? His present name is Nahumi which, to my ears at least, sounds every bit as good as Hoch. Obviously there has been some misunderstanding, and I'm sorry for it, and if I have done anything to distress you I am sorry for that too, but he told me that he thought he had met Father. He didn't say a thing about meeting you, and I think I may be forgiven for presuming that if he had met you the experience would have left a fairly permanent mark on his memory.

But in any case why should you feel personally affronted? I had merely asked him to pay a courtesy call on Berthold, and also convey my greetings to you. What makes you think that I regarded him as a prospective suitor? To be sure, I had hoped that you who know so much about music and the arts might care to show him something of London. He is a fine and richly cultivated man who is spoken of highly by everyone in Bor Shachor, even Celeste (who, as you know uses praise sparingly), and although it may be true that he does not display the greatest discernment in dress, and that his memory (like mine) occasionally tends to wander, it is, if I may say so, a little uncharitable to dismiss him as 'a dishevelled heap of senility'. It would never have occurred to me that he was Berthold's age. He doesn't look it, doesn't act it, and, even if he was, that doesn't make him ready for the knacker's yard. I know that age is regarded by young people as a crime, but it often carries certain qualities which people of my generation at least were brought up to respect, and one of them is sagacity. Nahumi is a good, calm and wise man and I say all this not because I am anxious to press him upon you, but because I fear you have misjudged him.

I don't know what he was like as a young man. If you say he was a miser I'm prepared to take your word for it, but I think I must point out that not everyone has the good fortune to be brought up in a wealthy family, and when you say that he haggled over a cup of coffee he may simply not have had the money. I would not call him a prodigal spender even now, but life-spans increase while incomes diminish and one has to husband one's resources carefully. I can only say that I know him to be generous in every important respect, which is to say with attention, with time, with concern. Gerald dashes off cheques in all directions, but never has a minute for anyone, and as he himself says, he's a miser for time. I am not sure that I don't prefer the misers for money. There is, in any case, all the difference in the world between being careful and being a miser and people who may count every penny they spend on themselves often spend fortunes on their wives and children. He happens to be a man with few needs. I can only hope that the tone of the letter you sent to me in no way reflects the manner in which you received him, otherwise I shall be unable to face the poor man. There is, however, no point in exchanging recriminations, so can we let the matter be forgotten? We shall be in England shortly and as you can imagine both Celeste and I are looking forward eagerly to seeing you and it would be unfortunate if anything arose between us which might spoil the atmosphere of Father's celebrations, or which might add to poor Berthold's burdens.

Your loving brother,
Henry

Dear Berthold,

I appear to have dropped a clanger. All I can plead in mitigation is that I meant well, and if by chance they could have taken to each other it would, I think, have been an ideal match for all concerned. I didn't know his name had been Poetzhaendler. I certainly hadn't the slightest recollection of the fact that he had stayed with us in the Saltzkammergut in 1931. Still, it could have been worse. *He* might have turned *her* down and where would we have been then? But I have learned my lesson and I hereby vow that I shall not henceforth recommend to the attention of Gwendoline Victoria Hoch, spinster, of Fetlock Hall, Fetlock, in the county of Essex, any male, eligible or otherwise. But what does one do with her? Had we been of good Catholic family she would no doubt have entered a Convent and would have been a Mother Superior by now, or more likely, have founded her own order. Had we been among the haute bourgeoisie of Anglo-Jewry she would, I suppose, have reconciled herself to being single, and possibly even of taking a lover, but we exist in an odd little nook of Jewish society, neither *haute* nor *petite* but rather muddled-middle, where people get married and that's that. They may, indeed, no longer stay married, and among our children's generation, of course, divorce is so frequent and widespread that it has become a form of licensed wife-swapping (with hefty cuts for the lawyers), but not to have been married in the first place is almost unheard of, and that's why one hears those snide little titters about Matthew. People are

less unkind about Gwendoline, though come to think of it –
you don't think *she* could be? Do you? I mean, she *does* want
to get married, doesn't she? Pardon me for asking an absurd
question, but one reads such fantastic revelations (we get the
English papers here) about the most sober-seeming individuals
that one is no longer certain about anything, even one's own
sister.

While on the subject of Matthew, did I tell you that he has
become a more or less permanent part of the Gittleson household, even to the extent of becoming a member of their cham-
ber ensemble? Gary has resigned his piano to him (Matthew
was always, of course, an accomplished player) and has taken
up the 'cello. They go on trips together to the seaside and
Matthew tutors the boys in Latin and Greek, and rumours
abound as to the sort of lessons he's been giving Mrs Gittleson
which are in direct contradiction to the rumours I have mentioned before, though Celeste, who sometimes reads the most
sinister implications into the most innocent situation, says: 'It
may be a front.' As for myself, I find the situation neither
seemly nor wholesome, though I will say that he drinks less,
and if he doesn't, he shows the effect of it less. Did I tell you
that the Gittlesons are sending both their boys to Clifton
merely because Matthew went there? I didn't, of course, tell
them, and neither I presume did he, that he was sent down
under a cloud (not the usual sort of cloud, of course, but cloud
enough for poor me – 'he's Matthew's brother', nudge, nudge).

I mention all this not to win your sympathy or to show
that while you have our Gwendoline there, we have our
Matthew here. Ten Matthews drunk don't add up to one
Gwendoline sober, but we are not an easy family. I am glad
that you at least have Alice beside you and that Father is
controllable. I need hardly add that I am looking forward to
seeing you all.

Gerald is here but we've seen nothing of him yet. I took
a taxi to meet him at Lud, but the driver made a detour to
avoid a traffic jam and got lost and I arrived at the airport in
time to see Gerald being driven off in a huge limousine. I
then received telephone messages from the King David Hotel
to say he was coming to see us, then further messages to say

he was being delayed, then he finally arrived while we were out, and by the time we returned he was gone. Matthew, who got a quick glimpse of him, said he looked as if he was about to blow a fuse. So far he has spent most of the time in conference with government ministers, departmental heads, industrialists and bankers, and I don't know whether he's buying Israel or selling it. I am told he got Father a priceless Byzantine urn for his birthday. Father may like Gerald, but he hates bric-à-brac and will probably break it over his head.

This is probably my last letter before our flight. The boys are meeting us at Heathrow and we shall be spending the weekend with Stanley before going on to Fetlock.

Yours ever,
Henry

Dear Berthold,

A quick note to tell you Celeste will not be coming. No, no, it has nothing to do with her health (which has never been better). Gerald is with us and he expressed an interest in the villa next door about whose future we have heard all sorts of rumours. We introduced him to Michaeli, our lawyer, who made some inquiries and discovered that it was no longer available, which did not surprise us. What did surprise us was the discovery that it is to be demolished to make way for a new block of flats. 'Over my dead body,' said Celeste, which is why she's not coming . . .

Henry

Chapter 3

Family Reunion

Dearest Celeste,

We are safely at Fetlock Hall. Father is fine and in good spirits, and, rather more surprisingly, so are Berthold and Martha. Gwendoline has, I think, forgiven me for the Nahumi fiasco and all send their love and regret you cannot be with us.

Our journey, as you must be aware by now, did not quite work out as planned. Humphry kindly offered to help with our luggage, but when he arrived bearing his own suitcase, and dressed in a striped suit with high padded shoulders, a jacket almost down to his knees, a broad-brimmed hat and two-tone shoes, I suspected that he regarded his role as that of more than mere porter, and when he sought to check in his baggage along with ours it was plain that he was labouring under some misunderstanding. Then it occurred to me that perhaps he was going to Europe of his own accord, except that he didn't have a ticket.

I don't remember asking him to come to England with us, do you? And I scanned my memory for something I may have said which may have given him the impression that I did. I do recall asking him whether he had ever been to England, and he said no, and I further asked him if he would like to go, and he said yes, but that surely, even with his gift for reading into language meanings it doesn't contain, would not lead him to presume that I would pay for his ticket. Anyway, there he was all dressed up with suitcase in hand and nowhere to go, and about him a crush of something like fifty relatives who must have come specially to see him off.

At the same time, Matthew, who should have been waiting for us at the airport, failed to appear. I phoned his home, phoned you, the Gittlesons, and began wondering if I should phone the hospitals or police. Anyhow I didn't, for if he was in hospital he wouldn't be catching the plane anyway, and so I waited, then phoned again, then had him paged, and when he still failed to materialise, managed through explaining that he was a Very Important Person – an ex-Colonial Governor (fibber that I am – we of course travelled BEA) – to have the flight delayed. And when he failed to appear even then, I quickly transferred the ticket to the waiting, perspiring Humphry, amid the cheers of his relatives, and he is with us here, two-tone shoes, striped suit, sombrero and all, in Fetlock. You can imagine the looks we got when we arrived, especially at his pointed, two-tone shoes. Father took him for Matthew and asked if he thought he had come to a fancy-dress party.

If Berthold is not too pleased to have Humphry here, he is infuriated with Matthew. 'His action is unforgivable even by his deplorable standards.' I suggested something might have happened to him. 'It does all the time but not to come to Father's centenary, even after I'd paid for the ticket, is the last straw.'

Rodney is here, safe and well, for which God be thanked, but beyond that there is little I can tell you about him which will add to your peace of mind.

Stanley and William are both well too, though naturally distressed that you failed to come, even though I explained why. They both admire your determination, but Elaine felt a little put out and said that you will go to any lengths to avoid seeing your grandchildren. They all came to the airport, bless them, all anoraked and jeaned and long-haired, so that I was not quite sure who was which or, indeed, whose, though I hope I gave the right present to the right child, and even if I didn't they were all pleased with what they got. (Incidentally, do you remember saying about the time we left that all those long hairs were a passing fad? Well, they're not, you know, in fact they're longer than ever and I am ashamed to say that I was not quite certain who were my grand-daughters and who my grandsons). Stanley and Elaine made me very comfortable though, I thought, with excessive care, as if I was a decrepit antique which might fall apart if mishandled, and although it is supposed to be midsummer they provided me with both an electric blanket and hot-water bottle, and made extreme efforts to see I was undisturbed, to the point of leaving me in almost complete isolation for the two days I was there. (Humphry, by the way, stayed with William. I gather that he put the bidet to a use for which it was never intended, but otherwise there were no complaints.) Elaine has turned Greek, both in dress and hair-style, which suits her, and in cooking, which doesn't suit me. She can't serve up a sausage without wrapping it in vine-leaves and on the second day of my stay I nipped out to the Great Western Hotel for a plate of kippers (and I hadn't gone for more than half an hour before she sent out the children to look for me).

They also helped me into my chair and out of it, and rushed to my side every time I was about to ascend the stairs, and by the end of my stay I began feeling every bit as decrepit as they thought I was.

The festivities begin formally on Sunday with a service of thanksgiving to be conducted by the Chief Rabbi and various puisne clergy. Berthold has erected a cathedral-sized tabernacle on the lawns, large enough to take a congregation of five hundred, and beside it a refreshment marquee.

Martha misses you. She said you are the only member of the family she can talk to, though from what I can see she's been talking non-stop from about the moment we arrived. Gwendoline said it was just like you to put a ruin, and an Arab ruin at that, before your own family, and the trouble with you is that I had over-indulged you from about the day we got married. Father hasn't commented on your absence, but that's possibly because all women above a certain age look alike to him.

Martha doesn't quite know what to make of Humphry, whom she has lodged with the servants, but who joins us – invited or not – at meals. He had Gwendoline enthralled with tales of his war-time exploits on behalf of the Allies in North Africa. 'They should have given you a medal,' she said.

'Impossible,' he said, 'is all very secret.'

Martha keeps looking at him and at me, and concluding, I suspect, that I brought him along to throw a spanner in the works. 'I know he's your gardener,' she said to me, 'but people don't usually invite their gardeners to family celebrations,' to which I explained that in Israel one doesn't have to invite people; they come unless they're specifically told to stay away. I can tell you of one person who was definitely happy to have Humphry around – Miss Naysmith – but here I venture onto the margins of low gossip and must say no more. Miss N is the only surviving servant of the pre-war or, indeed, the post-war years and Martha treats her with rather greater deference than any of her relatives, but then it is easier to find relatives than servants these days, and infinitely easier to keep them. Martha tells me that she has such a rapid turnover of staff that she almost pays as much in commission to the agencies as she does in wages. I suggested it might be an idea to pay higher wages. Wages have nothing to do with it, she said, for no matter how much she pays, the staff leave as soon as they learn English, and apart from Miss N the only servant to have been here longer than a year is the butler, a deaf Moroccan.

The general atmosphere as we are waiting for the fun to begin is one of solemn chaos, and I escape from time to time to the Fox and Hounds which remains as it was when I first set foot there one evening at the age of sixteen – even to the old dog slumbering by the open fire. I presume it isn't the same dog, and if it is he's been stuffed, but everything else is unchanged. Would it not be nice to have something like the Fox and Hounds in Bor Shachor? . . . It could do well. Our savings are shrinking and our responsibilities are not diminishing, and it would be nice to have a source of income, would it not? Did you know that Martha's brother is a director of a brewery company? He didn't either, but they took over a bankrupt investment trust and found the brewery among the small change. Perhaps we can persuade him to set up a pub in Bor Shachor.

I know you laugh at my idea of opening a liquorice allsorts factory in Israel. All the materials are available locally, and although I know nothing about manufacturing sweets, I am sure Bassetts would be prepared to send one of their people out to set up the plant – a small one of course – and train staff, and to give me a franchise. They could do well out of it. Berthold thinks it could work and is prepared to invest a thousand or two and I think I could induce Nahumi (who has a good few marks salted away) to do the same so that I would hardly be risking anything at all. Berthold says he doesn't know anyone in Bassetts, but he does know Parkinsons (the humbug people). Can one get humbugs in Israel? Perhaps we could produce them too. Anyway, once the celebrations are out of the way I hope to use my stay here to come back with some ideas for a worthwhile investment. I know I look my age and sometimes feel it, but I don't think I should be, and frankly I can't really afford to be, living in complete retirement.

The whole show, by the way, including the marquee, is going to cost several thousand and Martha keeps complaining that we shall all be ending our days in the poor-house. If my prosperity should ever equal her poverty I shall die a fairly contented man. Berthold has not consulted me about the outlay so presumably he will not be expecting me to bear any of the expense. On the other hand I shouldn't like him to think I'm tight-fisted or destitute. Should I volunteer to pay a share of the expenses and, if so, what?

Berthold pulled me aside today and asked me if Humphry had a dinner jacket. I said if he had, he had never worn it in Bor Shachor, but did he need one? 'Yes,' he said, 'if he insists on being at dinner tomorrow night, which I take it he will, unless you can persuade him otherwise.'

Have you news of Matthew? We are, of course, all very annoyed with him for not turning up, but with time our annoyance has been changing to concern for we have received no word of apology or explanation from him. His telephone is either out of order or, what is more probable, it is disconnected because he hasn't paid his bill.

'Why the hell don't you go to the police and have it finished with?' said Gerald, though of course going to the police doesn't finish anything and could well start something. I know so little of Matthew's private life that I'm always slightly apprehensive of where he might be found and in what circumstances. Berthold seems to share my feelings and we are not taking any action on the matter until the festivities are over.

I am, as you must have gathered, enjoying my stay and look forward to the celebrations, but I do wish you were here, my dear, not only to share my pleasures, but because one does feel a little odd to be unpartnered at a family reunion – at least in our sort of family. The animals round here (with the exception of poor Gwendoline) all come two by two, which, by the way, may be the reason why Matthew chose to stay away; his nerve may have failed him. Family reunions are really roll-calls, aren't they? There's a tacit stock-taking of who is here and who has passed on, who are together and who are apart, and the single tend to be regarded with a mixture of commiseration, despair and, I suppose, impatience by the doubled, for they spoil the familiar pattern of pairs. I should like to stay on here for another few weeks yet and, although we must watch our expenses, it would be nice if you could join me for at least part of my stay because I am not at all happy at the thought of you being in that house on your own.

All my love,

Henry

Dearest Celeste,

I can't believe it, and neither does anyone else. If it's true, it will, of course, settle one issue for good. Matthew decidedly is interested in women, even if he has discovered his interest a little late in life. But surely it can't be true. It doesn't go with what one knows of him or, indeed, of Nicky. Does she know how old *he* is? Does he know how old *she* is? She is, or at least she can be when she dons a dress and runs a comb through her hair, a fairly, perhaps even very, attractive woman, but he was, after all, a daily guest in their house, enjoying their food, their drink, their hospitality. Did he have to enjoy her as well? One was aware of Matthew as a fairly dissolute character, but I would not have thought him capable of such base betrayal. I was, of course, aware of the rumours, but then I am aware of many rumours, and anyone who thinks there is no smoke without fire has never lived in Israel, and certainly not in Bor Shachor.

Who has custody of the children? And where are the happy pair living, and on what? Has she private means, and if so, can she keep him in the manner to which he thinks he should become accustomed? Berthold used to send him a small monthly stipend to supplement his pension, but he may have it stopped if what you say is true. No one, of course, has said a word to Father, but no doubt he'll find out.

How is poor Gary taking it? He used to think of Matthew as everything a man should be and even described his drinking habits as 'a cultivated foible – to show that he's also got faults'. Will he regard his escapade as a further calculated foible? He's such a nice man, Gary, but such a sad one. Hasn't he the sort of personality that invites misfortune? Every time I see him I want to put an arm round him and say: 'Come now, things aren't all that bad.' But of course they are. Could he have second sight? Is he still sending the boys to Clifton?

What does she see in him? Granted he's a well-preserved man for his age, but he's an aged man and were it not for the fact that she was already married to a prosperous American I would have suspected that she was after his pension. I am told that young wives of a certain age are prone to all sorts of escapades, but surely not with a man old enough to be their grandfather? Perhaps she's seeing him with Gary's eyes. So much for opting out of the rat-race. Or is this perhaps the final opt out?

But to turn from one calamity to another. The centenary celebrations went off very well, but for the fact that the centenarian who was the occasion of it all wasn't there. In other words Father has taken another of his turns. Last time he dug in his heels, you will remember, he insisted he wasn't a day over ninety-two; now, through a different method of computations, he has worked out that he is only eighty-four, at which rate he should soon be restored to middle age. And, as before, as soon as Berthold tried to reason with him, he dived under his bed-clothes and stayed there. This time even Alice's efforts proved unavailing, and he is there still.

The celebrations, of course, had to continue as planned, and Father was hardly missed. Indeed not a few of the guests mistook Berthold for Father and congratulated him on his youthfulness. Still the service of thanksgiving sounded eerily like a memorial service and poor Father was spoken of in terms that are not usually heard of a man in his lifetime. It was sheer obituareese, and when they had finished I almost jumped to my feet to say *kaddish.*

Ring and Bryhmer, as usual, catered the reception and the fare was what one might expect at this time of the year – melon, salmon mayonnaise, strawberries and cream. The place was black with Rabbis, which meant that we had kosher champagne and, although I love almost everything about Israel, I do not love its champagne, or whatever it is they put in champagne-style bottles. I'm afraid I did a rather naughty thing, raided Berthold's private store of Chablis and had some of that.

Everybody's been asking after you and I was stopped by various dames in large hats who engaged me in conversation on how we had settled down, and how brave they thought we were, and how they would have liked to have done the same thing, but didn't have the courage, or where they did have the courage they didn't have the money. It's nice to know that people think we're still rich.

Gwendoline got merry on the pseudo-champagne and was leaning rather heavily on Humphry's arm, who looked a little troubled by the burden, as well he might.

There was a dance in the evening and we were hoping Father might come down, because, as you know, he always takes great pleasure in watching the growing daughters of the family in festive array, but he could not be induced to stir even for them. I asked Berthold if he should not perhaps call a doctor, especially as there must have been about fifty medicals among the guests.

'No,' he said, 'he has embarked on a war of nerves.'

But to get back to the new generation of daughters. Again, I am never quite certain who is whose, but they were all as pretty as a flush of tulips, and there were a particularly beautiful pair of sisters, tall, blonde, with the carriage of

Maharanees, who entranced everyone and gave off a sort of sunny coolness. And whose were they? Gerald's. I know Alice is beautiful, but Gerald must have had some share in them and it is difficult to think that a portly little Hebrew could have sired such wenches.

I nearly had words with him at one point when he turned to me and said, 'Who's that scruffy little pip-squeak dancing with my daughter?' For the pip-squeak turned out to be our Rodney, who had, predictably enough, arrived at the Hall in a sweater. Did you know, by the way, the dinner-suits have changed colour? When I was a young man, if you went to a good tailor and you kept your shape you could wear your dinner suit for life, but now they're in brown and green and violet and dinner shirts have blossomed out in every shade under the sun, so that if someone does arrive in an improbable outfit one is no longer certain whether he is not introducing a new style. Gerald himself was wearing a broad cummerbund (which may, however, have served as a corset) and a shirt with frilled ruffs like a Restoration buck. He's been on the long distance phone from the time he came. Do you know that he has three watches on his person, one giving the London time, another New York and the third Los Angeles, though I am not certain that he always knows which watch gives what time. I asked him why he didn't relax, and he said : 'When you get to a certain level you've gotta keep juggling, otherwise you'll have the whole caboodle come crashing down on top of you.' Alice keeps telling him he works far too hard, but he doesn't take advice – though he does take pills, different colours and sizes for different occasions, and different times of day. He's already had one mild coronary which sensible people take as a warning to ease off, but it spurred him on. 'I've got a lot of unfinished business,' he keeps explaining, and adds : 'It's not for myself I'm doing it all – it's for them,' meaning his daughters. 'They don't look as if they need your money,' I told him frankly. 'It helps,' he said. 'I want them to do better than their mother.'

The young men one sees these days, within the family and without, are so unprepossessing that if I had growing daughters I would be worried – not that I get all that much joy from

our growing son. I had a long talk with Berthold last night
about this very problem. Duncan, his youngest, has turned
into another Rodney and what makes it rather worse is that
he happens to be a good bit older. Rodney is (correct me if
I'm wrong) twenty-two, whereas Duncan is twenty-seven and
has never been in any one job, or, for that matter, any one
place, for more than a year. I asked B why he didn't take him
into the company. They do so many things that there must be
something which would be up the boy's street, and he replied :
'It's a public company, I can't do that to the shareholders.' I
reminded him that Edward had also been troublesome. 'But
not at Duncan's age,' he said. 'What saved him was his two
years in the army.' It might have been the making of Rodney
too. Pity they don't have National Service any more.

I have often thought of cutting off Rodney's allowance, but
these youngsters seem to be part of a moneyless international
and live out of each other's pockets. I suppose if all the parents
involved were to cut off funds at once it might have some
effect, but a parent acting in isolation is helpless and in many
cases the fact that a son needs money is about the last link
one has.

There was a time when a young man could be made to
come to his senses by landing a girl in trouble, but nowadays
girls have the means to keep out of trouble, and even if they
don't they can get out of it, besides which the trouble itself is
no trouble. 'They're doing all the things we were afraid to do
because they can get away with it,' Gerald said to me, and I
almost told him to speak for himself. Not that I can see
Rodney landing a girl in trouble, he's too inert even for that. I
suppose I could get reconciled to his idleness, his tendency to
drift from job to job, from situation to situation if it came
with a certain *joie de vivre*. Your late brother, Anthony, was
an idler, but he got so much out of his sloth that I sometimes
came to wonder what I was getting out of my industry and,
as he put it, he never had time to apply himself to the business
of earning a living because he was so busy living, but Rodney
– like so many of his contemporaries – is such a miserable-
looking youngster. He talks with contempt about 'wage
slavery', but most wage-earners that I come across look a good

deal more cheerful in their slavery than he does in his freedom.

Now for some good news. Helene is with child, or possibly even with children, for she arrived in a striped billowing garment like a silken gazebo. Only she could have worn such an outfit without looking bizarre, and I had to hold her at arm's length to kiss her, which I did French fashion, on both cheeks, as if presenting a medal. I can kiss even Gwendoline with a certain spontaneous show of affection, but somehow anything one does about Helene assumes a formal basis, nor does one get the feeling on kissing her that human blood flows beneath her skin. Still, she's a pleasure to look at.

When I saw William in London he didn't say a word about her condition and Helene herself was wearing one of those voluminous dressing-gowns, and was, so to speak, hiding her light under a bushel. And as you yourself once observed, Helene in a dressing-gown is so different from Helene in a dress that one cannot always be certain that they are one and the same person. William, I'm afraid, is running to seed and is getting pudgy and placid and looks old for his years and I rather hope that the sound and the sight of a small infant scampering around the house may have a rejuvenating effect on him. Rodney certainly had that effect on me. Once the children start growing up and are away at school one does, at least I did, tend to relax into a sort of cosy obsolescence. At forty, one dreads the onset of middle age, at forty-three and forty-four one still fights it. By about forty-eight or forty-nine, with one's demi-century in sight, one resigns oneself to it – and it was then that we decided on Rodney. He was, if you remember, my dear, your idea, and after a false start or two, he finally materialised, our contribution to the post-war bulge. I was re-invigorated by the very sight of him and he gave us so much pleasure in his early childhood that we should perhaps overlook the disappointment he has become since.

Helene told me that she would have liked me over to stay with them, but they have the builders in. England too has its Patakoses, but, of course, she always has had the builders in, and hardly have one lot completed their renovations than another lot move in. It's like the Forth bridge. William, however, does not seem to mind and trails behind her at a respectful distance, beaming with proprietorial pride. She would have been the ruin of him if I had thought he was paying for her extravagances, but as it is she may yet be the ruin of her father, who, by the way, is at Fetlock, a dear little man, who obviously lives for his daughter.

Have you seen anything of dear Nahumi and, if so, has he said anything about the encounter with Gwendoline? Berthold told me that she was civil without being enthusiastic, but Gwendoline's civility can be more chilling than most people's cold shoulder and I hope it hasn't affected our friendship. He shares our strong feelings about the Seraglio building, and knows everyone. I think you should have him on your committee. I expect to be back in about a week and may have Rodney with me. I know he is passing through an anti-Zionist phase, but he has as yet not moved into an anti-free-ticket phase and he may spend the summer with us. The bait has been the Seraglio. I told him that you couldn't come because a building we both cherished was being threatened, and at that he sat up. I had touched on a password, ecology or environment or pollution, or maybe even all three, and something like a light came into his eyes and he wants to come over to help you fight the good fight. I do not wish to disparage his idealism, but if only young people would do half as much for their old parents as they're prepared to do for old buildings, we would all be living in a much happier environment.

I do miss you, my dear.

All my love,

Your
Henry

Dearest Celeste,

I take it Rodney told you the tragic details. I was too shaken to speak to you myself. A hundred years is a good innings by any standards, but Father has been so permanent a part of our lives that we got into the habit of thinking that he would be around for ever. What makes it all so particularly painful is the fact that by the time Berthold finally called a doctor the poor man had been dead for about two days, which means that even as we were gathered in thanksgiving for his continued being he had already ceased to be, and the five hundred guests who had only just dispersed from the celebrations had to be reconvened for his funeral. He was buried at Willesden next to mother, almost twenty years after her death.

Strange how she has slipped out of our reckoning, poor dear, as effaced in death as she was self-effacing in life. She was soft and tender and loving and scatter-brained (they say I took after her). Father was none of these things and used to get very impatient with her and I'm afraid he treated her rather shamefully. I wonder what brought them together. I suppose Father wanted to marry roots, which she had, and money, which she had, and pedigree, which she claimed to have.

Berthold has taken it all very badly, as if it was all his fault, but Father died of a stroke and when he sank under the bedclothes he was already dead. Neglect did not accelerate his end and calling a doctor would not have delayed it, though it would of course have meant that we wouldn't have been dancing downstairs while he was dying upstairs, but I am not sure if Father, who had a perverse sense of humour, would not have appreciated the irony of the situation. Martha, for her part, blames us, that is Gerald and me, for shrugging off all our responsibilities and leaving Berthold to cope with Father and his caprices, to say nothing of Gwendoline and hers. And in a sense she is right, but she overlooks the fact that Father had also passed over much of his money to Berthold as well as Fetlock Hall (which admittedly must by now be more of a liability than an asset). Still, this isn't the time for recrimination.

I suppose Berthold will now sell the Hall, which is a shame in a way for Father had hoped to establish it as an ancestral home to remain in the family through the generations.

Poor Father had, as with so much else, left it a bit late, for twentieth-century England was no place to establish an ancestral home or a dynasty and as he was setting up the upper classes were already beginning to sell out. If he had at least married into a county family his ambitions might have taken root, but mother, though of good Anglo-Jewish stock, was hardly county, and they were never really accepted by their neighbours. Still, he outlived most of the local gentry, and since the war he was about the only local resident with a place large enough for the annual church fête. He took pleasure in telling me that he – a pillar of the United Synagogue – was the biggest contributor to the local church restoration fund.

Martha has never liked the Hall and complains that the nearby marshes give off a vapour which is bad for her rheumatism. 'Young' Edward (who is almost sixty), the heir to the estate, has no sentimentality about the place whatever. I'm not sure that I have either, which does not mean that I would like to see it passing out of the family's hands. But who has the money to support such an edifice these days? And where can one find the servants even if one has the money? It would be nice if one could pass it over to the National Trust, but of course they wouldn't take it as a gift (even if it came with an endowment – which it wouldn't). Its main claim to fame, I think, is that it was among the first domestic buildings in Essex to have central heating and if it is not as old as or as distinguished as any of the more stately stately homes, it is infinitely more comfortable than they and, placed in good hands, it could make a first-class hotel. As such, I suppose, it would be worth about a hundred thousand pounds on the open market, but if Berthold could get planning permission to demolish the Hall and build a housing estate in its place, it would be worth ten times as much. That, I suspect, is what he will try to do, which means that there will not be one stone left standing upon another to indicate that the Jewish family Hoch passed this way. Sad, isn't it? Father was a Polish-born Jew with a German education who hoped to acquire eternal roots by hiding himself away in an obscure corner of England. And to this end he sent us all to good English public schools (Clifton, an Anglican foundation with a Jewish house was almost tailor-made for his needs), but he ploughed the fields and we scattered. Matthew hardly ever set foot in England from the day he came down from Cambridge. Gerald left for America almost as soon as he left school. I am in Israel. There is, of course, Berthold, but I wonder if he would have remained in

England if he had not been bogged down by his inheritance, and Edward, heir to the House of Hoch, is to make his home in Jersey.

If somebody had told me ten, or even five, years ago that I would have been content to leave England, I would have laughed in their face, but when we came to leave I left with hardly a pang. Of course I miss England, but the England I miss is no longer there. We did occupy a fairly cosy corner of Isleworth, but whenever we had to go somewhere we hurried forth with eyes averted from what was happening to the England about us. The best we can do now is to take some part of the England we cherish and try and transplant it in Bor Shachor.

Gerald is, of course, sufficiently American to be an incurable Anglophile, and he plans to buy a flat in London. 'I'm gonna be here two or three times a year, just to rebuild my sanity' – but the main reason is that Laureen is applying, in fact has got in, to Cambridge, and they're sending Amanda to a finishing school here, though I cannot conceive of anyone being more nicely finished. I asked him if he didn't feel tempted to buy the Hall so as to keep it in the family. 'Hell no,' he said, 'it's hardly older than me. If I was to buy a stately home, it would have to be Tudor or maybe even Plantagenet.'

He is full of remorse for not having visited Father more often, but Gwendoline is remarkably composed. She said that for the past decade or so Father had resented staying alive, and complained that we were keeping him going as if he were a prize exhibit or to establish a new record in longevity. He once told her that he would have disinherited Berthold if he had not already transferred his estate to him. (There's the insidious part about death duties. You start transferring your possessions to avoid them, and before you know what's happened you're at the mercy of your children. I sometimes draw comfort from the thought that I have so little left to transfer that I can face the prospect of death with equanimity.)

I cabled Matthew a ticket so that he could be here for the funeral, but he phoned to say he was too unwell to travel, and he sounded unwell. I hope it's nothing serious but it can be dangerous for an old man to take a young mistress.

I'm still upset at this absurd elopement, you know. One doesn't like to see one's brother make a a thorough ass of himself, but he has in fact upset our whole pattern of existence. You're troubled – as I am – about what they might do to the Seraglio, but what will happen to chez Gittleson now that the wife has flown? Neighbours aren't all that important in a place like Isleworth (or at least our corner of it) where everyone kept themselves to themselves, but they are important in Bor Shachor where neighbours are almost an extension of oneself. The Gittlesons were in and out of our house and we of theirs, and it was rather reassuring to have them beside us – especially with the Seraglio under threat – but now, with the wife gone and the sons about to go, Gary is hardly likely to remain. Empty buildings worry me, especially if they're next door. Damn Matthew and his ill-timed libido!

I know you'll think this sounds absurd, but I have the feeling that Berthold would like to live in Israel and would be happy with us in Bor Shachor. He continuously questions me about every detail of life there (as he did in his letters) and inquires after Gary and our other *dramatis personae* as if they were members of the family. He really hasn't much to do with himself here and now, with Father gone, he will have hardly anything at all. Becoming chairman of the company was really like being kicked upstairs to the House of Lords. But again it's largely his fault. He could have waited before passing over his shares to his sons. Still he had his photo in the papers with the annual report, and he is invited to the Lord Mayor's banquet and that sort of thing, which is worth more than all the money in the world to Martha. He gives a lot of money and she a lot of time to the right charities so he may yet get a gong. He deserves it, poor chap. Martha asked me if they give gongs in Israel.

We've been enjoying a typical English summer here, which is to say, it's cold and wet and I can't wait to get back to the sunshine and warmth and the cheerful chaos of Bor Shachor. Rodney will not, after all, be coming with me. He feels that I have been through enough with the death of poor Father and does not wish to add to my traumas for the time being, which is a charitable thought. I must say that I have been able to talk to him more easily in the past day or two and I suppose it takes something like a bereavement in the family to bring fathers and sons together. He is basically a nice lad, but he has an unfortunate habit of talking in slogans and I have the feeling that most of his generation have lost the capacity to think for themselves but get their ideas pre-cooked from some central soup-kitchen.

Incidentally, I have lost Humphry but am not trying too hard to find him, for frankly he was getting a bit above himself, which is something that everybody does in Israel, but it becomes a bit irksome here. He kept addressing everyone by their first name, even Martha. He called Gerald 'Gerry', which nobody does. Berthold has the unfortunate habit of relapsing into nursery talk and still calls me Podge, which Humphry picked up, and though I can just about take it from Berthold I shall not take it from Humphry. He was also, I thought, rather familiar with Gwendoline, who, for her part, did not do enough to discourage him and I suggested to Berthold – who of course sees nothing and hears nothing – that he speak to her about it. The climax of Humphry's presumption, however, came at the funeral when he took his place in a black suit and homburg (borrowed I know not from whom) among the front row of mourners, and one could hardly hear the Rabbi above the buzz of speculation as to who he could be, and it was widely assumed that he was a prodigal son born on the wrong side of the blanket, returning to pay homage to his natural father. The same thing happened at the Thanksgiving service when he sat down next to the Lord Lieutenant of the County in the area reserved for immediate members of the family and VIPs, and chatted incessantly about his war-time exploits, so that the Chief Rabbi had to interrupt his address till he quietened down. What I was prepared to overlook at the celebrations I could not overlook at the funeral, and I have not spoken to him since. If he does come back, you and I will have to be at pains to put him and keep him in his place.

I am sorry, my dear, that you've been unable to join me here, even for a few days. It would, as you said, have been an extravagance to do so, but I think it would have been forgivable, for I am a little lost without you, even in the bosom of my own family – indeed, especially in the bosom of my own family. I did intend to stay on for another few weeks to revisit old haunts, but what is haunting about the haunts is that we used to stay there together, and there is no point in seeing them on my own. I also hoped to establish some business contacts who might be interested in backing some ventures in Israel, but businessmen, even Jewish businessmen, do not seem to be particularly venturesome these days and, perhaps, I am not a Gerald and do not give the impression of a young man or, indeed, an old man who 'is likely to go places'. In other words, there is little to keep me here. This isn't the first time we've been separated but somehow since we've moved to Israel I find separations more worrying. Does that mean I'm growing (have grown) old? I only know I can't wait to get back.

All my love,
Your Henry

Chapter 4

Il Seraglio

Dear Berthold,

I hope you will forgive me for hurrying back to Bor Shachor when you have so much on your hands, but I feared that if I had stayed a minute longer I would have become a liability, for I tend to lose self-possession if I am away from Celeste for any length of time.

You are, of course, right. She should have come over for the funeral, but the moment she heard the news she was involved in her own crisis, and her reasoning – which I think is forgivable – is that while her presence at the funeral would have done nothing for poor Father, her absence from Bor Shachor could have done irretrievable damage to our neighbourhood. Let me explain.

There is, as I must have mentioned, a few yards away from us, a large and charming Arab house built in elaborate Moorish style, which is threatened with demolition, and Celeste and a few others quickly formed a committee to save it. They began sending letters to the press, drawing up petitions, drumming up publicity, but proceeding at a fairly leisurely pace, till they suddenly discovered, quite by chance, that the demolition men were about to start work and the day they arrived on site was the day of Father's funeral. Celeste, Gary, Nahumi and others quickly formed a human barrier across the roadway. A crowd collected (as crowds will in Israel), the police came out, and the fire brigade and the almost inevitable television crew. The longer the confrontation continued, the larger the crowd grew, and the size of the crowd was, of course, in itself an assurance that the wreckers wouldn't pass, and that day they did not. First round to Celeste and Co.

The next morning she and Michaeli (our lawyer) went to court and obtained a writ preventing the contractors from taking any further action on the site for ten days, which gave us a necessary breathing spell, but no more. They had permission to proceed, and, according to Michaeli, when they next came to court the permission could be confirmed. In short, if we wanted the permission rescinded, we would have to go to the people, or rather the tribune of the people, the mayor.

Are you still with me? Now Bor Shachor, like most towns in Israel, is not ruled by any one party but by a coalition of three or four. The ruling party here is the Workers' League, but it is kept in power by the Holy Alliance, and there, I thought, I had some leverage, for had I not just returned from Lock's of St James' with a bowler-hat for the Chief Rabbi? I called on him with the gift, which he tried on with shaking hands and was so lost in admiration of himself that for a while he forgot I was there. It was, I'm afraid, rather too large but he thought it did do something for him (though I wasn't sure).

'You must let me pay,' he insisted. I waived that aside and gradually drew the conversation to the question of the villa.

'Ah yes,' he said, 'your wife, women's liberation, eh?'

'It has nothing to do with it, all she wants – '

'I know, I know, but why she bothers – an English lady, the mother of children, a grandmother – it is not fitting.'

'The hat?'

'No, your wife. It is not fitting an English lady, a mother in Israel, mixes in such business. Is bad example. She starts nuisances and everybody follow.'

'She's not doing it for fun.'

'Why she's doing it? I ask myself, I ask her. Why she's doing it?'

'She wants to keep Bor Shachor beautiful.'

He looked at me blankly.

'She wants to keep Bor Shachor beautiful,' I repeated.

'Bor Shachor?'

'Yes.'

'Beautiful?'

'Yes.'

He put down the bowler and addressed me in Hebrew. He could no longer contain himself in English.

'Bor Shachor is a dung heap,' said he, quoting what sounded like scriptures, 'its women harlots, its men idolators. Nobody with sense comes here, anyone who comes to his senses leaves it. I don't know why you came. At first I thought you were fleeing from your wife. Then when I met your wife, I thought you were running away from the law, but they tell me you're an honest man.'

'I hope I am.'

'Then why did you come?'

'Because we like it here.'

'Here in Bor Shachor?'

'Yes.'

He threw up his arms : 'Englishmen!'

'So you see we have a vested interest in the place.'

'What's a vested interest?'

'We think this is a nice place and it could become a nicer place.'

'When the Messiah comes.'

I explained what they were trying to do with the Seraglio and why we were trying to save it.

'But save it? Why save it? It's only a building, an old building. A hundred years old. They pull it down to put up new ones – all the honour to them. They should pull down all Bor Shachor. And besides I'm only a Rabbi, Chief Rabbi, but a Rabbi. What can I do?'

'You have influence with the Holy Alliance.'

'Mr Hoch, the Holy Alliance is politics and politics is a delusion and a snake.'

'A snare.'

'A what?'

'Politics is a delusion and a snare.'

'Are you telling me what politics is? I was born with politics. I am living with politics. I die with politics.' His voice rose to a shout. 'Politics is killing me. But I don't dirty my hands with it.'

'But aren't Rabbis virtually appointed by the Holy Alliance?'

'Heaven forbid. Moses received the Torah on Sinai, and handed it down to Joshua, Joshua to the Elders, the Elders to the Prophets, the Prophets to the Men of the Great Synagogue, and the men of the Great Synagogue to the Rabbis.'

'And who are the men of the Great Synagogue?'

'Great men, but dead: they've been dead a thousand years.'

'So who in fact appoints Rabbis?'

'The Religious Councils, they should also be dead.'

'And who appoints the Religious Councils?'

'The Holy Alliance, the politicians, they should all be dead.'

'So couldn't you have a word with the Holy Alliance?'

'I don't mix the holy and the profane.' And he turned to admire himself in the mirror again.

'Nice, no?'

I next tried to see the mayor, who is, of course, head of the Workers' League and who, I discovered, was abroad on a study mission (a very studious lot the mayors round here), and was received instead by a deputy mayor, a small freckle-faced man with sandy hair, a ginger moustache, a small skull-cap and, surprisingly, an Irish accent, who greeted me with open arms and his secretary brought in orange squash and buttered bagels.

'I've been waiting for this privilege for months. I've seen you in synagogue and I was hoping for a chance to talk with you. I'm surprised you and your wife haven't joined the party.'

'Which party?'

'*The* party, the Holy Alliance, of course. I know the words holy and religion sound offensive to English ears, especially in a political context, but you're born and die in this country in a political context and you can't keep politics out of religion and religion out of politics, and sure do we not say in our very prayers, "The world and the fullness thereof are the Lord's," and if politics isn't of this world, what is? My friend

Mittwoch's been telling me that you're a regular worshipper at his synagogue, both on Friday nights and the Sabbath morning, but he didn't have to tell me, for English Jews, if they're Jewish at all, are traditional. Isn't the Englishman traditionalist by definition, and there's nobody more English than the English Jew abroad, and so of course when I heard you were here I said to myself, ah, new recruits, new strength, allies. The one thing I didn't expect from you and your good lady was opposition.'

I asked him what he meant.

'Listen, don't misunderstand me. Don't think I don't admire her, but what she's trying to do now I've been trying to do for half my life. I too want a beautiful Bor Shachor. What do you think I'm doing in a God-forsaken hole like this? I'm an M.A. and LL.B. I won the O'Malley medal in Law at University College, Cork. If I had gone to England instead of Palestine, I could have been a Queen's Counsel, or a High Court Judge, a Knight maybe. I'm here because I want to make it a paradise, and by Jaysus, I will.'

'Then why demolish the Seraglio?'

And he rose to his full height, which must have been about four foot six, pulled a roll from a rack and unfurled it across his desk.

'There you have the answer,' he said with a wave of his hand. 'The Bor Shachor master plan.'

'I'm afraid I can't read blueprints.'

'You can't?'

'No.'

'Don't you think you should learn before you try to upset the work of a life-time?'

'I know what a tower block looks like and I wouldn't care to have one in my back garden.'

'There's more to the plan than a tower block or two. We're building a city, and what we're doing is not only for Bor Shachor. It's for Israel, for the whole Jewish people, for eternity. This is a poor country, you know. It hasn't enough oil to charge a lighter, no gas, no coal, not even a decent-sized peat-bog. Its principal vendible asset is sentiment. Jews may not want to live here, but they're prepared to buy property here –

or at least in places like Nathania or Herzlia. They haven't exactly been running to sink their money into Bor Shachor, but that's going to change. I've found an investor who is prepared to create a posh quarter. He'll be putting up a block of flats which will be the last word in luxury and raise the image of the entire neighbourhood. Your villa will double in value – no, it'll treble, quadruple, quintuple. You'll be able to sell the site for a million, and move into a penthouse flat – '

'We don't want to move into a penthouse flat, we're not interested in a million, we like our villa.'

'Right, right, I appreciate that, but think of your children. I mean look at me. I've nothing to gain out of life. I was born into a prosperous family. I had a rich father and I shall be leaving penniless children, but one thing I will have is a place in history, I'll be to Bor Shachor what Dizingoff was to Tel Aviv, what – what – '

'Romulus and Remus were to Rome,' I suggested.

'Exactly. I'm going to put it on the map. I'm not only working to put towers in the air. I got this archaeologist organising a search in the ground. He's a bit of a stickler for facts and hasn't come up with anything exciting yet, but I'm going to give this place roots, a history, sanctity, character. Did you notice all the new buildings are being finished in the same shade of cream? I have a slogan for the place: "Bor Shachor, the cream-coloured city half as young as time." How's that?'

I was not impressed.

'Look, you and your wife could be at the foundation of it all, the founding father. You'll have streets named after you, Hoch Highway. No, you'll probably want to Hebraise your name, Hoch, that's Govoha. Nice name, Govoha – Govoha Boulevard. Do you know what I've done to my name? Oh, it's clever. I was born Dan Kolb. Kolb is Yiddish for calf, the Hebrew for calf is *Egal*, so I now call myself Don Egal. In other words, Donegal. How's that, eh? You've got to turn Israeli to be proper Irish. Now what was I telling you?'

'You were digging for history.'

'Ah yes, yes – and I'll find it, and if it isn't there, b' Christ, I'll put it there. The world will ring with the name. It'll give the people a new image of themselves, a feeling of civic pride,

the knowledge that they are citizens not merely of some face-
less, shapeless, colourless huddle of boxes, but of a pearl among
cities. I am giving your wife an opportunity, which I do not
offer lightly, the chance to be a partner in this historic venture,
and not to obstruct the inevitability of the inevitable.'

'I don't think Bor Shachor is without character now –'

'It's nothing to what it will be, and I'm starting from the
ground up. In fact, as I said, I'm starting below ground. Just
you wait till you see what my archaeologist digs up.'

'But why look for history below ground when you have it
above?'

'The Seraglio you mean? It's not an ancient building, it's
not even old. It was built by some lecherous Turk just before
the First World War.'

'But it's got distinction.'

'And do you think the flats won't? They'll be the tallest
buildings between Tel Aviv and Cairo. You'll be able to see
the Mediterranean from the top floor. And it won't be just
one great big rectangle set on end. There'll be Moorish trim-
ming along the top. I've got one of the best architects in the
country, my own brother-in-law, working on it.'

'It'll stick out like a sore thumb.'

'To start with maybe, but there'll be others like it. We'll
have a whole concourse of high-rise buildings, a new town
hall, a university – '

'The University of Donegal.'

'No, no, I still hope to be around, and I wouldn't want
things named after me in my life-time – it's immodest, but it'll
come – a university and a technical college. In fact, we have
the beginnings of a technical college in our school of printing.'

'A cathedral, maybe?'

'Well, there aren't enough Christians in the vicinity for that,
but I have plans for a synagogue, and for an underground
railway – I don't want the place cluttered up with cars and
buses like Tel Aviv. And it's not only bricks and mortar I'm
thinking about. Last year I had the privilege of laying the
foundation stone of a new Yeshiva. It'll have places for five
hundred students before it's finished and become a place of
pilgrimage for Rabbis and Talmudists from the world over. It

already has a hundred Rabbis and students in residence and I take a walk beside it in the evenings just for the sound of their voices chanting the ancient chants, arguing over this line of the Talmud or that. It fills my eyes to hear them. I'm no great scholar myself but the next best thing to learning is providing others with the opportunity to learn. My father, rest his soul, was a fine scholar, and although he was a successful businessman, if you went into his office, you'd find this great big volume open in front of him. Ah, you would think, the ledger, but it was a far higher book of account – the Talmud. If he was only alive to hear them, Yeshiva students, in a place like Bor Shachor! And they marry early, you know, these Yeshiva boys – at sixteen, some of them – and have Catholic-sized families, ten, eleven, even twelve children. Within a few years they'll fill the town. You won't recognise it. I'm going – ' his eyes glowed as he spoke – 'I'm going to make Bor Shachor a holy city – the Limerick of Israel.'

I returned crestfallen to Celeste. 'The man's suffering from megalomania,' I said.

'That's alright,' she said, 'they all do, it's the local disease. I suppose it came over them after they got rid of malaria. But we'll manage.'

I am glad you've found time to enjoy a brief holiday with Martha, and your picture postcard of the greensward at Frinton brings back happy memories. We haven't had a chance to have a holiday this year so far, but you know when it gets to July or August one doesn't get the compulsion to get away at all costs that one does in England, partly, I suppose, because the unbroken sunshine gives one – or at least gives me – the feeling that one is on holiday all the time, but we should like to explore the country a little, and once our anxieties about the Seraglio are over, we hope to get away to the Galilee for a few days.

Yours ever,
Henry

Dear Berthold,

I wonder if I could ask you as a matter of urgency to find out what is happening to Humphry and where he might be.

He hasn't written home (I am not even sure if he can write) and his relatives are accusing me of abduction and are threatening to call the police.

I am sorry I have no hard news of Matthew. He and his consort are on honeymoon in some place or other, Italy, I believe, but other than that I can tell you nothing. I presume he is better, otherwise he would hardly have been able to travel.

It's a strange affair. Can you imagine what would have happened if anyone had run off with your wife or mine? But Gary is perfectly calm about it, even – though I know this sounds ridiculous – even proud that his wife should have found so noble and distinguished a lover and he talks about it like a father whose daughter has made a particularly good match. I never could understand Americans, and I certainly cannot understand Gary. His boys are to go to Clifton as planned and he will be travelling with them to England in September.

I know this may sound crazy to you (and in truth it doesn't sound all that sane to me) but do you think there is any point in introducing Gary to Gwendoline? Yes, our Gwendoline. He is not divorced yet, but divorces here are a formality and no doubt once he has established the exact whereabouts of his wife he will take out the necessary papers. In some ways they would be well matched. He is as affable as she is tempestuous. He is, if anything, too affable and if you ran him down in a bus he would apologise for being in the way. He has her love of music. He is, or at least was, fairly well off. There are, however, obstacles and it would be best to face them at once. First of all, he has been everywhere and lived everywhere, and sees Israel and, in particular, Bor Shachor, as his home – 'my final resting place' as he put it – and has sworn to live nowhere else. I can, in certain circumstances, imagine Gwendoline leaving England, and possibly settling in Israel, but I cannot imagine her making her home in Bor Shachor. Can you?

Secondly, Gary is a Reform Jew and is the mainstay of the local Reform congregation. We have been over this before in the matter of Nahumi, with the important difference that while Nahumi was, so to speak, a fellow traveller, Gary is the leading light, or, as he put it, 'I'm in this for real.'

Finally, and most crucially, there is the matter of age. I don't know exactly how old Gary is, but he has all his own teeth (as do most Americans – they're rather good on teeth, Americans), but on the other hand he served in the final stages of World War II (in the *Marines*, would you believe it?), so that he must be at least fifty and even that would make him more than ten years younger than Gwendoline.

On the other hand, he has a deep admiration and veneration for everything English, and although I would not say, in all charity, that Gwendoline is a perfect example of the perfect English rose, she did go to Cheltenham Ladies' College, is a member of the Fetlock Hunt, is a good horsewoman, and no-one who had met her or heard her would ever guess that her father was born in a Polish ghetto. But what would, I think, clinch the matter as far as Gary is concerned, is the fact that she is Matthew's sister. He already feels a link with Matthew through the fact that he has run off with his wife, and if he could marry Matthew's sister it would bring him closer still – about as close as he could be without marrying Matthew himself. For such a possibility he would, I believe, overlook their age difference and would, I think, be prepared to move to England, and once in England he could be shown that the United synagogue embraces all types, the ultra-Orthodox, the Orthodox, even Reform Jews – provided, of course, that they do not flaunt their reformist convictions, and Gary, I can assure you, is no flaunter. Besides, one of the things he loves about England is the English love of tradition (I need hardly add that he hasn't set foot in England for over a decade) and it would not, I think, be difficult to convince him that the Reform movement, while natural to America, had no real place in England.

I am thus fairly hopeful that Gary could be induced to view the idea with favour, but what about Gwendoline? She complained that Nahumi was old enough to be her father (which of course he isn't), but I am not sure if she would prefer someone who, comparatively speaking, is young enough to be her son.

As a matter of fact, Gary is at this very moment involved in a battle on behalf of the Reform synagogue, and Celeste, who has become a glutton for causes, had adopted it as her own. Gary's villa was far too large even for his entire family, but now that his wife has left and his sons are about to leave, he has moved into a flat and wants to convert his villa into a Reform synagogue. It would mean removing a wall which separates two downstairs rooms, the enlargement of the kitchen to contain a canteen, the provision of toilet facilities, etc., but all within the context of the existing building. The facade would be untouched, but hardly had his architect completed his sketch before he received two orders, the first to declare that the villa was of outstanding historical and architectural importance, and that not a stone of it must be touched without permission from the relevant authority. The other was that the area was designated exclusively for residential use and the villa could therefore not be converted into a synagogue.

It was obvious to anyone with half an eye or, indeed, with no eyes at all, that this was a device to kill the Reform synagogue before it started, but Celeste leapt on the first order and rushed to the town planning office. If Gary's villa was of such outstanding historical and architectural merit that one could not even touch the interior, she demanded how was it that they planned to demolish the Seraglio which was built on much the same lines and which was, if anything, even older.

The official was ready for that. First of all, he explained, Gary's place had interior grills which were the work of a famous Egyptian artist (which, he said, the Seraglio hadn't). And secondly, it was precisely because they were demolishing the Seraglio that they found it necessary to slap down a preservation order on the villa. And he added for good measure:

'Do you know what would happen if the house became a Reform synagogue? They're nearly all Americans, the Reform Jews. They all have cars, and they all travel on Shabbat. Your street would become a parking lot.'

'Couldn't you have "no parking" signs?'

'What Israeli motorist pays attention to signs? They will park in the roadway, they will park in your garden, and if you didn't have steps, they would park in your front hall.'

A delegation consisting of Celeste, Nahumi, Gary, Michaeli and myself then waited on the mayor who was still away on a study session and we were received by my friend, Donegal. As always, Celeste was the spokesman.

'Let's come clean,' she said. 'You know and we know that the orders slapped on the villa have nothing to do with preservation, or designated areas, and everything with the fact that they propose to use it for a Reform synagogue.'

'Oh, I wouldn't say that.'

'But I would.'

'It's dangerous to jump to conclusions. That villa has grill work by a famous Egyptian artist, Abu – '

'And it has a water-closet by a famous Barrhead engineer, Sankey, but you're not going to tell me that it's of greater architectural interest than the Seraglio.'

'Perhaps not, but the Seraglio is much bigger and would cost a fortune to preserve, and in any case the Seraglio is going, we have to keep an eye on what's left – '

'Then why were we allowed to pull our villa inside out, it's almost an exact copy of Mr Gittleson's – '

'Did you – ? You had no right to. You should have applied for permission and had you applied you wouldn't have got it, for it's a listed property. I am not even sure that you're not liable to a fine for making conversions without a licence and we could ask you to restore the building to its original state, but – ' and he broke into a smile as large as his face – 'we'll not make a fuss over that. After all we all have the interests of Bor Shachor at heart, so let bygones be bygones. The fact that you have, as you say, pulled your own villa inside out, is all the more reason why we must take care to preserve Mr Gittleson's. Then, of course, there is the character of the area to be considered. That quarter, as you know, is designated as a first-class residential area – the only one in Bor Shachor – and you wouldn't want to ruin your own amenities by having a synagogue in the same street.'

'It wouldn't bother me,' said Celeste.

'Have you asked your neighbours?'

'I have,' said Gary. 'Half of them belong to the Reform movement as it is.'

'I belong to three synagogues,' said Donegal, 'but I wouldn't want to live within earshot of any of them. It's your interests I'm protecting. I am not trying to interfere with your religious rights. I'm a deeply Orthodox Jew myself but I respect other denominations. Speak to the Mother Superior of the Little Sisters of Mercy, or Sister O'Mulihan, they'll tell you.'

'You wouldn't let us rent a school hall,' said Gary.

'Who?'

'You.'

'Me?'

'The municipality.'

'When?'

'On the High Holy Days.'

'Sure, but that was for security reasons. You could have some gunman slinking in among the worshippers, then hiding himself in the building till the children came in the next morning. We couldn't risk that.'

'If I am not mistaken,' said Nahumi, 'you let school halls for weddings.'

'Do we?'

'I am sure.'

'Then I'll have to put a stop to that – though as you know there are so few places in Bor Shachor large enough to take a wedding party that we cannot be too strict. We can't stop all jollification in the town, security or no security.'

'If we had a synagogue,' said Gary, 'we wouldn't need to hire school halls, and what's more we would let it out for weddings. The paucity of decent public buildings is one of the reasons why we want to build a synagogue.'

'Wait a bit,' said Donegal, 'and you won't recognise the place. In another few years we'll have the new residential area, and a new class of resident, hotels, a new town hall – '

'Would ze town hall be available for Reform services?' asked Nahumi.

Donegal waved his neat little hands, 'That's, that's all in the future. Who says I'll be around then? I can't speak for my successors.'

'Then speak for yourself,' said Celeste, 'would you allow a public building to be used for Reform services?'

His smile faded. 'Look, you came here to discuss building

permission for Mr Gittleson's villa, and I explained why it couldn't be granted. If you should want to debate theology, by all means. Come to my home one evening and we'll discuss it over a cup of tea, or maybe something stronger, but – if you don't mind – not during working hours.'

'Mr Donegal,' this was Celeste again, 'you will forgive me for saying so, but I detect a hint of intolerance in your attitude.'

At this he raised himself to his full height.

'You talk to me about intolerance? Was Longbow tolerant when he landed in Ireland? Was Cromwell tolerant?' and he launched out upon an extended course in Irish history at the end of which Celeste and I were left feeling almost personally responsible not only for the massacre of Drogheda, but the Irish famine.

'We go to court,' said Michaeli.

In the meantime the court has come to us in the form of a writ requiring us to desist from blocking the approaches to the Seraglio or from otherwise interfering with the movement of vehicles in the area.

'What happens if we ignore it?' asked Celeste.

'We go to jail,' said Michaeli.

'Now wouldn't that be an interesting experience?'

Nahumi, however, didn't think so, 'Ze law is ze law. If we do not like it we have it changed in parliament and not in ze street.' And Gary more or less agreed with him, 'You spoil a good cause with bad tactics.'

'Doesn't everybody break the law here in one way or another?' said Celeste.

'All ze more reason why we don't,' said Nahumi. 'The court says we desist, we desist.'

'You mean that we should pull out and let the wreckers in?'

'What else?'

On which rather forlorn note I must end.

Yours ever,
Henry

Dear Berthold,

Thank you for the news of Humphry which I have passed on to his relatives who, however, do not seem entirely assuaged: they want some definite proof that he is alive and well. He appears to have been the main support of an aged mother and I suspect that she is looking to me for a subvention until such a time as he returns. It might be worth my while to pay it if only to make sure that he doesn't.

In the meantime I can set your mind at rest about Matthew. The prodigal son hath returned, yea, even with the prodigal wife, which is not to say that they are as yet wife and husband, for they had their honeymoon first and are to marry later. It is usual, of course, to do things the other way round, but given Matthew's age one can understand his hurry. He had been slightly indisposed, but now looks tanned, well, hale and hearty. 'Just what the doctor ordered,' he said, without, however, specifying exactly what it was that the doctor did order. Whatever it was, it appears to have done him good, and if the idea of Nicky and him running away together seemed bizarre when I first heard of it, they do not look too improbable when seen together hand-in-hand like a pair of newlyweds.

He appears to have shed weight and years and, unless I'm imagining it, he has gained height. And Nicky has suddenly matured into full-blown womanhood, like a tightly-closed, wind-blown tulip opened by a sudden burst of sunshine. She had everything to attract, the eyes, the teeth, the neck, the bosom, the shape, without quite adding up to an attraction and there was something in her manner which gave one the feeling that the world was due to come to an end in twenty minutes. She is now more relaxed. She was also a rather sickly white in spite of the constant sunshine. She is tanned now to a burnished brown and has broadened out too (though not, I think, with child – though come to think of it, why not?). How long is it since I saw them last. Two months? Three months? I have never seen such a transformation in two people in so short a time. In the case of Matthew the effect is partly due to good tailoring. It is true that, as he liked to claim, he went to the best tailor in Saville Row, but it is further true that he hadn't been to a tailor since before the war, and one usually found him in mouldering tweeds which always threatened to come apart, and which sometimes gave off an offensive odour. He has now returned with a complete new wardrobe, the work of an Italian tailor, and he received us in an immaculate white tropical suit, the like of which I hadn't seen outside the pages of Somerset Maugham. Where, I wondered, did the money come from? Not from me, nor, I take it, from you. He certainly doesn't have it himself, so it appears that he is not only acquiring a wife with beauty, youth and character, but also a fortune.

'I regard myself as fairly fortunate,' he said to me. 'The pity of it all is I didn't meet Nicky thirty years ago.' To which I retorted, 'Thirty years ago Nicky was about five!'

Gary, would you believe it, gave a home-coming party for them and was so pleased with the appearance of his wife that he was almost tearful. 'She's a new woman,' he kept saying, 'a new woman.' One might, in the circumstances, have thought that he would want to hold on to her, but he has already begun divorce proceedings – which are a mere formality here and only take a matter of days – and no doubt he'll be arranging the marriage as well. One is, of course, very happy for Matthew, but it all seems a little unreal, even unseemly.

Celeste, by the way, doesn't think that Matthew has changed all that much, but that I had built him up in my imagination as a seedy old drunk because I like someone to be sorry for. Methinks the good woman has been reading too much psychology of late. Still, that's Matthew settled (more or less) and one perennial source of anxiety may be struck off our agenda. Which brings me to the next – our dear Gwendoline.

I asked Gary if he had any plans to remarry and quoted Dr Johnson about 'the triumph of hope over experience', but he said, 'No, no, I've had a happy marriage. If I could find another Nicky I'd marry again tomorrow.' How's that for charity? Gwendoline is not, of course, another Nicky nor, indeed, another Nicky twice removed, but the fact that he is prepared to marry again is, I think, hopeful and I hope you will do your best to introduce them when he is in London next month.

All is not over in the Seraglio war and, indeed, it looks as if the fight is only just about to begin. Celeste and I were walking recently on the outskirts of town when we came upon a thin, withered bespectacled figure in a pith helmet, grubby vest and voluminous shorts scratching away in a ditch and muttering to himself.

'Looking for something?' I asked.

'Yes,' said the figure, without looking up, 'the past.'

We had chanced upon Donegal's dig.

The archaeologist introduced himself as Potemkin, '*the* Potemkin', he added and Celeste and I made the appropriate noises though neither of us had ever heard of him. 'They have dragged me out of retirement to dig my own grave. I am alone here. The men stop before they start or stand around leaning on their spades and arguing among themselves. I am given no budget, no staff, no understanding, they hardly pay me anything, and they stand over me waiting for me to unearth a Tutenkhamun.'

'Mr Donegal – ' I began.

'Mr Donegal should fall into a hole and stay there, so should the whole town council, so should Bor Shachor. If they had given me a free hand I might have come up with something, but the only part of the area which could have something, I mustn't touch – '

'Which part is that?' asked Celeste.

'Quolboyeh, the old town, where the villas are, but they're planning a new housing site just at the back and if I should find anything it could delay things – '

'Was there something in Quolboyeh?'

'People say there was – I, Potemkin, I am not so sure. I have written a paper on the subject in the *Levantine Archaeological Review*, a copy of which I by chance have in my jacket – only by chance I have left my jacket at home. I leave everything at home. I leave my watch at home. What time is it?'

'What were you saying about Quolboyeh?' said Celeste.

'I, Potemkin, I am not so sure there is anything there. You

see it is a hill, a *tel*, and everybody who thinks he's an archaeologist thinks a *tel* must be as full of history as a rice pudding
is full of rice. No so. No so – not Quolboyeh, and I am Potemkin, I know what I say, but even if there is nothing there is
more there than I will find here. Here there is absolutely
nothing. There, there is relatively nothing – '

'They why are they afraid to let you touch it?'

'Because even where there is nothing there is always bones.
People have been fighting here for five thousand years. The
whole country is a graveyard. Everywhere bones, and bones
mean trouble.'

'But why?'

'Because the country is full of ignoramuses who think they
know something, especially archaeologists. Everybody who
digs a hole in the ground thinks he's an archaeologist, so if
they find a bone, even from a dead chicken, they begin writing up papers to show they've discovered the remains of Titus,
or Saladin or Alexander the Great, or perhaps all three, and
if they're Jewish bones you can forget about the whole thing –
your work never starts and your troubles never finish.'

'What's so special about Jewish bones?' I asked.

'They're Jewish, that's what's special – '

'But how do they know they're Jewish?'

'They don't, but that doesn't stop the bearded idiots from
rushing in from all corners of the land and shouting holy,
holy, holy, don't touch, the soil is sacred.'

'I don't understand.'

'What is there to understand? When an Arab's been dead
for thirty years, then he's dead and done with and he becomes
dust unto dust, but when a Jew dies, then, according to tradition, his life only begins. He goes on forever. You cannot move
him, and you mustn't touch him. In other words, if bones are
trouble, Jewish bones are endless trouble, and as they don't
want trouble up there on the hill, I am digging down here in
the valley. A plague on Donegal.'

I don't know if it was a coincidence (from the look on
Celeste's face I suspect it wasn't) but a few days later a work-
man repairing a sewer pipe near the Seraglio unearthed a
human skeleton. Within minutes the place was teeming with

policemen, Rabbis, Yeshiva students, Potemkin. It is not yet established whether the remains are Jewish or not, but in either case it will be at least a fortnight before any workmen are allowed on the site and a lot can happen in Israel in two weeks.

Celeste and I hope to snatch a week or so – circumstances permitting – for a holiday in Sfad, which, as you know, is high up in the hills of Galilee, and is comparatively cool at this time of the year. We have asked Gwendoline to spend the High Festivals with us, but she hasn't replied, and I wonder if I said something, or failed to say something, which might have upset her. Could you ask her if she's coming?

Yours ever,
Henry

P.S. I've received a fairly dusty reply from Bassetts. Do you think there is any point in writing to Parkinsons?

Dear Gwendoline,

You can't be serious! I read and re-read your letter, as did Celeste, and the only conclusion we could reach is that you are suffering from the after-effects of poor Father's death and and that you are too over-wrought to know what you're doing.

Does Berthold know of your plans? For if he does he has given no hint of them in his letters. All he had to say was that you were happy, cheerful and collected. He was obviously trying to reassure me. A parent's death, no matter at what age, is always a great trauma, and I was a little apprehensive as to how you would take it. Now I know.

The first thing I must plead with you is not to take any irreversible step, otherwise you may be doing something which you may regret for the rest of your life. Humphry obviously has qualities which were lost on Celeste and me, but even if he is everything you believe him to be, I hope you will forgive me for pointing out a few irrefutable facts.

I am not sure how old Humphry is, but from what I can gather he was a schoolboy at the time of the American landings in North Africa, which means that he cannot be more than fifty and may well be nearer forty, and although you look young for your years – Alice observed that you look younger every time she sees you – I hope you will forgive me for pointing out that you are rather more than that.

You mention in your letter that 'Lady Burdett-Coutts of the banking family married an American forty years her junior'. But first of all you are not Lady Burdett-Coutts; second of all we are not a banking family; third of all Humphry is not an American; and finally, had I been Lady Burdett-Coutts' brother, I would have advised her against it.

You are also a woman of some education and attainment. He – admittedly through no fault of his own – has none. I am not even sure if he can read, and whether he can or he can't the fact remains he doesn't. Moreover, although I would not make exaggerated claims for the antiquity and prestige of the House of Hoch, we do enjoy a certain standing both within the Jewish community and without. Nor is it irrelevant to point out that Berthold's wife is *née* Holtzhacker, that Celeste is *née* Koch, that Matthew is a CBE and was within an inch of becoming a Colonial Governor and a Knight, that Berthold is a liveryman of the Cordwainers' Company and I, though not in the habit of flourishing my small claims to fame, am a JP.

Of Humphry's family I know nothing. I never even knew that he had any at all till they descended in their hundreds to see him off at the airport. They included a large number of women, who could have been cousins, sisters or wives. All I can tell you about him is that he is a man of some energy and not a little enterprise and although I would not go so far as to say that no house should be without its Humphry, he was fairly useful to have around – which does not, however, mean that I would either commend or welcome him as a brother-in-law.

You will notice that I have not uttered a word against him, my only objections to your proposed plans being that I cannot see you, with your upbringing, sophistication and literary and cultural tastes, settling down with someone like our mutual friend. I can see quarrels, recrimination, grief, perhaps even bankruptcy. I am not, of course, suggesting that he wants you for your money, but presumably, if you marry, he will have some control over your affairs, and there is no knowing how he will handle them. I know that you have gone through unhappy, even tragic, times, but in the last resort Father looked after you and you have always been spared financial worries, and financial worries – as I am beginning to find out – are worrying.

Finally, I know how sensitive you are to outside opinion. Aren't you a little afraid that you might become a laughing stock?

You have not said what Humphry would do for a living, for although gardeners can earn a good wage nowadays I doubt if he could keep you in the manner to which you have been accustomed.

You could, of course, forswear your comforts, but there is no indication that you plan to do so, which means that he would be living on your income. And where would you live? How would you live? What would be your milieu? A thousand questions arise which you have not attempted to answer.

But perhaps I am exciting myself unnecessarily and that by the time you receive this letter you may have come to your senses; if so, please forgive the tone of the foregoing, for although we have had our occasional differences, we have always been a close family, and my only concern is for your happiness.

Your loving brother,
Henry

Dear Berthold,

I was writing to you about Gary when I received the bombshell from Gwendoline. I tried to phone you both but got no reply. Have you sold the Hall already? If so, where are you to be reached? I read her letter and re-read it and still haven't quite taken it in and, in so far as I have taken it in, I can't believe it. *Humphry as my brother-in-law?* I'm sorry, I can't believe it. Some spinsters, when they reach a certain mature age, reconcile themselves to their position, but Gwendoline apparently grows more desperate with the passing years. How else can one explain her choice? What can she see in Humphry apart from the fact that he's a male? I know she's beyond the age of consent but I think I can rely on you to be firm with her and confront her with the realities of her situation and, above all, impress on her that whatever she does do she should do nothing which cannot be undone.

There is, however, some hope to be drawn from the most unfortunate circumstances and it occurs to us that if she is so desperate for a man that she is ready to accept even Humphry, then there is every chance that she would be willing to accept Gary, even if it meant marriage in a Reform synagogue, and settling in Bor Shachor. You have not met Gary, but you have met Humphry and you can take it from me that man for man the former is the more probable and certainly the more satisfactory choice. I have spoken to him about Gwendoline in general terms and in fact about our whole family and he is looking forward to seeing you all. He will be in London with his boys next week and will phone you as soon as he arrives. It would be nice if you could invite him down to the Hall – provided of course it is still in your hands – for a weekend and it may not be too late to introduce him to Gwendoline at even this eleventh hour. There is nothing that so much commends a man to a woman than the fact that he is interested in her, as I think he will be. Moreover, he is – unlike our squat, neckless friend – a fairly well-formed man, and not at all bad-looking, though he exudes a sort of moist earnestness which some people find off-putting. I can only tell you – as you will no doubt discover for yourself – that he is a thoroughly good man in the best sense of the word, but even if he was without the many qualities I know him to possess, Gwendoline may still be drawn to him, for it seems to me that a woman who can fall for Humphry will fall for anyone. Will you prepare her for the visit? He is a Yale graduate, by the way, and his family (on his mother's side) has lived in America since 1848. His mother was a Stettinger. This means nothing to me, but it may mean something to Gwendoline, who was always a keen student of pedigree, which is another reason why I find her choice so incomprehensible.

Do you think Humphry could have cast a spell on her? You will no doubt think the question absurd, but he has a static eye which shows occasional flickerings of life and the effect is slightly unnerving and Celeste once said she had taken a liking to him because he reminds her of an illustration of her favourite nursery tale – Rumpelstiltskin, but then if he has such power why use it on poor, misguided Gwendoline?

It does look, does it not, as if we're a family of late developers. First Matthew, and now her. I'm beginning to be a little bit afraid for myself.

Please answer as soon as possible. I have not slept since I received her letter and I shall not be sleeping till I've received yours. I draw passing moments of consolation from the feeling that all this is not really happening, that I'm asleep and it's a dream.

Yours ever,

Henry

Dear Gerald,

You may well ask. In a word – a pimp. I might have written in greater detail if you had taken the trouble to answer my letter, but I do not regard a cable with the words WHO THE HELL IS HUMPHRY QUERY as worthy of a substantial reply.

Henry

Dear Berthold,

I'm at a loss to comprehend your attitude, and I can only conclude both from your sentiments and the tone of your letter that, like Gwendoline, you too are over-wrought by Father's death. What do you mean 'there's no point in arguing with Gwendoline'? There is every point in an issue like this. Do you happen to know who or what your prospective brother-in-law is? I didn't, although he has been in my employment for over half a year, partly because I was afraid to find out, and partly because I liked to think of him as a sort of rude, primeval Jeeves. Well, I have since been startled into making some inquiries and the following is a portrait of the gentleman who – unless you and/or I do something about it – is about to become our brother-in-law.

Born in Meknes, Morocco, 1928 (which makes him forty-

six, or sixteen years younger than Gwendoline). Educated in
Alliance Israelite Primary School. Left home at fourteen.
Arrested in 1943 for pilfering from American army stores and
again in 1946 for dealing in stolen goods. Moved to Israel in
1949. Joined Israeli army. Invalided out in 1950 after losing
the sight of one eye in a crash involving a stolen army vehicle.
Would have been court-martialled, but for his injury. Arrested
in 1952 for smuggling sheep over Jordanian border and trading with the enemy. Married in 1954. Arrested in 1955 for
keeping a disorderly house. Divorced in 1956. Fined in 1957
for illicit currency dealing . . . and so on and so forth even
unto this day, though in fairness I should add that in the
seven or eight months that I've known him he has not been
involved in anything illicit, or if he has he has never been
caught, but I think you will agree that he is less than a model
citizen.

You ask if I have any greater joys to offer Gwendoline,
but do you know of any greater disaster? In any case I think
Nahumi, even if he was the miser she says he is (which he
isn't), and even if he is as old as he looks, would have been
better. And Gary, of course, would have been a superb match
but of course, we have left it too late. I say 'we', but the fault
is really yours. You were on the spot, you could have (or at
least should have) seen the way things were going, and that
if you were helpless to stop them you could at least have delayed them, and even if you couldn't delay them you could
have sent out some warning, so that I might have tried to
get Gary to London a little earlier. I am glad you agree with
my high opinion of him, but as you say, it is too late now.
On the other hand, you are far too ready to reconcile yourself
to failure. Can you imagine what the marriage will mean?
Can you see it lasting? I can't and if it breaks down – as it
inevitably must – I dare not think of the consequence. Hitherto, through all her many disappointments she has always
emerged with her fortune and her sanity intact. In this case
she may lose both.

I am not at all reassured – as you seem to be – to learn that
Humphry has enrolled in a hotel management course. Is she
planning to take over the Savoy or Claridges? Or will she

depend on his extensive experience to open a *Maison Tolerée*?

Does Martha know? I should imagine she would have Gwendoline committed if she did, and for once she would be right.

I will grant that Gwendoline is something less than a thing of beauty and a joy for ever, but with all that she is obviously a person of quality which Humphry as obviously is not, and I can only think that you are prepared to go along with her preposterous schemes because you see it as the only way out of your own dilemma. Let me hasten to add that I am not blaming you, that I might have done the same in your position and that – as you have more than once hinted – I may have settled in Israel because Gwendoline is in England. You've had her on your hands for so long that you are ready to welcome any prospective suitor, no matter how improbable, as a redeemer – especially now that you are about to sell the Hall and there is the chance that you might have her on top of you in your new home. You have borne so much for so long that you are entitled to any relief even if it should come in a form as improbable as Humphry. My only complaint is that Humphry is no solution. You will have her back on your hands after a month, certainly within a year, and in pieces.

Now you may say – and if you won't Martha will say it for you – that it's alright for me to proffer such advice from the safety of Bor Shachor while you have to cope with the traumas as they arise. Let me therefore suggest the following. Our house is a two-storey affair. I have discussed the matter with Celeste and we are prepared to add a third storey – even at the risk of having Patakos among us once more – for the exclusive use of Gwendoline, entirely self-contained with its own staircase, though she would, of course, be free to use the rest of our house as her own. All this would, of course, take time (given Patakos it could take an eternity), but we have a spare room (with bathroom) even now, which she would be free to use till her own flat is ready. In the meantime can I rely on you to dissuade her from any irrevocable act?

There is one final point which I am reluctant to broach but I think we must realise between ourselves, that whatever

Humphry sees in Gwendoline her money cannot be the least of her attractions. I don't know how rich he expects to become out of the marriage, but of course whatever he gets Gwendoline would have to come with it, which makes me think that he might settle for a lump sum which might be less than he expects but which would have the advantage of coming unattached. I see the financial papers here and I'm aware that the company is passing through unhappy times. I also know that you have had heavy outgoings on the centenary celebrations, but it should not be too difficult, if you bring Gerald into the affair, for us to buy him off. I'm willing to contribute my share and more than my share.

You can tell Gwendoline what I said about Humphry – every sordid detail – though not, of course, what I said about her.

Yours ever,
Henry

Dear Gerald,

I don't know what Berthold has been telling you, but if you know your brother you'll appreciate that he would find it difficult to utter an unkind word about Herod. Let me not go into too much detail except to say that Humphry is a squat, one-eyed felon, without background, breeding or education, and a police record the size of the Magna Carta. He was at Father's ill-fated centenary celebrations and sat right beside you on a number of occasions. I can't understand how you could have failed to notice him. Does the enclosed photo refresh your memory? He is the blue-chinned figure with the bow-tie under his ear, one eye staring into the camera and the other down your wife's cleavage. Would you care to have him as your brother-in-law?

I have no doubt he is after Gwendoline's money and I am reasonably certain that he would prefer a small fortune without Gwendoline to a large fortune with her, and I suggested to Berthold that he make an offer accordingly (we would, of course, all share in it, according to our means). A perfectly reasonable suggestion, you would say, would you not? He didn't even reply, but wrote to Celeste instead to ask if I was alright, for although my letters were written in my hand, they did not in the least sound like me. I knew that Berthold was many things, but it never occurred to me that he was – to use an apt phrase I have picked up in Bor Shachor – such a *shmock*.

May I therefore turn to you? I know you're busy, but it isn't every day that you are threatened with the prospect of a Humphry for a brother-in-law. Could you not fly over to London and handle the matter in person?

Yours,
Henry

Dear Gwendoline,

You are probably right. I do lack charity and imagination and it is probably to the credit of Humphry that given, as you say, 'his unhappy start' he should be 'the sweet, gentle, understanding creature he is'. I should perhaps add that these were not qualities which were glaringly evident during the time he was here, which does not, however, mean that he does not possess them. You are also more familiar with the works of the Rabbis than I am and it may well be true that what a man was is less important than what he is, and that his direction is more important than his origins. It must certainly sound good in a sermon, but it does not always work out quite that way in life where a past record is usually a fairly safe guide to future performance. That, at least, has always been the case with horses, but it may be different with men and if both you and Berthold aver that Humphry is a new man, then who am I to contradict you? But even if he is a new man, and even if you should become a new woman, that – if you will forgive me for saying so – will not close the gap between your years, nor the problems which would arise out of your different backgrounds, nor the cynical titters which would go on behind your backs. I repeat that I am not suggesting that he is marrying you for your money, but I think we should face the possibility that your fortune may have entered somewhere into his consideration, and if he is not marrying you for your money he probably would not marry you without it. I fear

I may have put that rather crudely, but you are the only sister among four brothers, and if I should appear unduly protective, it is because Berthold is so preoccupied with winding up Father's estate that he possibly did not give your affairs the attention they deserve. I can also now see that Celeste and I did not choose the most opportune moment to make our home in Israel. We could have reasonably waited till Father was dead, except that it would have been a rather morbid thing to do and, besides, in spite of his great old age, he might have outlived us, or at least continued till a time when it would have been too late for us to go. Celeste is sixty, I am seventy, and it was really either then or never.

There is, however, no point in going over the past. I am rather more concerned about the immediate future. You say you plan to marry as soon as Humphry has completed his hotel course. When will that be? Where do you plan to live? The Chief Rabbi has always presided at all our family weddings (to say nothing of the funerals). Have you spoken to him about your plans? I am relieved to hear that you have not as yet made a formal announcement of your engagement. Could I ask you to leave the matter in abeyance for another few days? I feel that the whole issue is too important and too delicate to be dealt with adequately by letter. I have to be in London next week in connection with Father's estate (it looks as if the lawyers will be getting more out of what's left of it than the Chancellor of the Exchequer or us) and we can have a heart-to-heart talk about the whole affair from beginning to end. As you see, I am no longer really trying to dissuade you from your course, I am only asking you not to hurry. I hope the information I sent to Berthold about Humphry didn't upset you, but I thought it was useful for you to know the facts. Father always said (with more than a hint of irony in his voice) that you had the best head in the family and although I reacted with a certain amount of panic when I first heard your plans, I am now perfectly confident that, as Celeste put it, 'Gwendoline would never do anything really foolish.'

Your loving brother,
Henry

Dearest Celeste,

The world is full of surprises, some less pleasant than others. I had just boarded the London plane when who should I find beckoning me to a place but the Deputy-Mayor, Donegal, en route to Europe on a study mission. And the first thing he asked me as I clicked on my seat-belt was: 'Do I owe you *maazeltov*?' I pretended not to know what he was talking about. 'Your sister's engagement, I mean.'

'How did you know?'

'These things get about, besides, there isn't all that much good news around that you should want to hide any little bit that comes your way. *Maazeltov* again.'

'It's not official – '

'Official, unofficial – she's going to marry him, isn't she?'

'I'm not sure.'

'You mean not if you can help it? I know the inquiries you've been making – '

'I made them in the strictest confidence.'

'And I heard about them in the strictest confidence. I can understand your feelings. Didn't I go through the same thing with my own sister, the apple of my father's eye, the child of his old age? He didn't have too much time for us, the boys in the family, but lavished everything on her, music lessons, ballet, a Dublin finishing school, nothing was too good, and no one was good enough for her and she remained a virgin – of sorts – till she was thirty. Then she comes on holiday to Israel, falls in love with a Bokharan road-sweeper and wants to marry him – a savage-looking character in baggy trousers and a turban. She always had a romantic streak, and I suppose she took him for Sinbad the Sailor. When father heard about it, he screamed "over my dead body" which is exactly what happened. He dropped dead and a month or two later they married.'

'Didn't you try to stop them?'

'Try? I moved heaven and earth. I tried to speak to her, but sure I was wasting my breath. She's woman, Irish and Jewish. Anyone of them is bad enough, together they're impossible. I then tried to bribe him. He took the money, but thought it was a wedding present. Then finally I got somewhere – I found he came from a remote mountain village which was isolated from the rest of the Bokharan community and I found a Rabbi to put it about that the Jews in that village were perhaps not quite kosher, and of course, with that floating around I didn't find it too difficult to persuade our local Rabbi not to marry them. I couldn't get away with it for good, of course, but I thought it might hold up things till she came to her senses.'

'And?'

'She's got pregnant, so that settled that.'

I pondered on what he told me over lunch and after lunch and then I asked him: 'Are all the Jews from Morocco automatically accepted as Jewish?'

He saw what I was getting at immediately. 'But what would be the use? It's not as if they're in Israel. I've no pull with the British Rabbinate, have you?'

'That isn't the point. When they apply for the banns, the London Rabbinate will make inquiries in Israel, and if they should be told that Humphry – '

'And supposing she gets in the family way?'

'Not my sister.'

'Don't be so sure. My sister went to a Convent school, and what with that and a good Jewish upbringing we thought she was safe for life. I don't know your sister, but in the last resort she's a woman.'

'But a woman in her sixties.'

'Ah.'

'Exactly.'

'In which case she's hardly in a position to pick and choose.'

'You seem to think that any marriage is better than none.'

'I don't, but she obviously does, and if I was you I'm not sure that I'd stop her.'

'Do you know Humphry?'

'I've heard a thing or two about him, but sure no one's perfect. If you want to make your home in Israel, you'll have to stop thinking in terms of dynastic marriages. We're a mixed-up race, and the bigger the mix the better.'

'You didn't think so when your sister was involved.'

'No, but then my sister wasn't sixty. Think about it.'

But of course I had thought about it – I have thought of nothing else since the news broke and I told him I wasn't looking for blue blood, or even a gentleman. I had even ceased to think in positive terms. All I wanted was a male of Jewish parentage and without a criminal record. Was that too much to ask? He agreed that it wasn't, and he promised to help.

The plan, briefly, is this. There is, he said, an element of doubt about the antecedents of many immigrants and he believes he can sow sufficient doubts about the matrimonial entanglements and antecedents of Humphry to delay matrimonial proceedings by six months or even a year, and a lot can happen or unhappen in a year.

In return, I undertook to make a generous donation to any charity of his choice or to party funds, but he waved it all aside. 'No, no,' he said, 'I want no reward. I remember what I went through with my own sister. The knowledge that I can spare a friend from going through the same will be sufficient recompense.'

The plan would not be a particularly dignified way out of our predicament, but I am sorry to say there is no other, for the first thing I discovered when I reached Fetlock was that Gwendoline's plans were accepted as a *fait accompli*, not only with resignation, but with something like relief. Berthold had not tried to talk her out of it at all, but had merely put certain questions to her which he thought she must ask herself before taking such a momentous step, and even Martha, whom I had expected to be aghast at the thought of having Humphry in the family, said with a grim little smile playing about her tight little lips: 'He is a rough diamond, but no doubt Gwendoline will smooth away his rougher edges,' and far from opposing the marriage, she, Martha Hoch, née Holtzhacker, has given it her blessing. Does that not surprise you? It surprised me, till I discovered the reason – the happy couple are to settle in Israel, and not only in Israel, but in BOR SHACHOR!

There is much more to write, but I am exhausted from the journey and I want to catch the last post.

All my love,
Henry

Dearest Celeste,

Everything's been happening at once.

First of all, old Grosskopf is dead! He's been handling our affairs for as long as I can remember and one would have thought somebody would have told me. He died of a stroke a month ago, and when I called at his office I was confronted with his son, a pasty little lad with a neat parting and large glasses. He seemed to know what he was doing, but I was too shaken to know what I was doing, so the meeting proved rather inconsequential. I don't know why I should have been so shaken, except that Grosskopf was my exact contemporary at Clifton, and I suppose his sudden death was a rude intimation of mortality.

The second surprise came a little later. I was standing in Gray's Inn Road waiting for a taxi when a familiar face sailed by in another. He must have noticed me as well for the taxi suddenly braked then reversed and who should step out but Matthew?

'Henry?' he said a little uncertainly.

'Yes.'

'Thought it was a damned near likeness. What are you doing in London?'

'Seeing my solicitor. And you?'

'Ditto.'

'Aren't you supposed to be getting married or something?'

'Was, but some sort of complication's cropped up.' He didn't elaborate, but you know it wouldn't surprise me if he had a wife and children hidden away somewhere, for what better complication than a family? Also something of the glow about him when he returned with Nicky has faded and he's out of his white linen suit and back into tweeds. (Nicky, by the way, is in New York.)

We travelled down together to Fetlock on the 4.15 from Liverpool Street. I had the return half of a third-class ticket which I was determined to use and he bought a first-class ticket, but still got in beside me.

'What's the point of travelling third-class on a first-class ticket?' I said.

'Buy first-class as a matter of habit – it's immaterial where I sit.'

'Rather a waste.'

'Yes, I suppose it is.'

'You don't have to sit here just for my sake, you know.'

'I prefer to. Do you mind?'

I asked him if he had heard about Gwendoline.

'Yes, splendid news.'

'Do you know Humphry?'

'Met him. Splendid fellow.'

'Do you know anything about him?'

'Gather he's got a bit of a past. Haven't we all?'

'Speak for yourself.'

'I have not, as yet, seen anything of Humphry. Obviously he's trying to keep out of my sight, and with good cause. There is, however, one thing which I have established. We are not faced with the meek surrender of the pathetic infatuation of an elderly spinster for a gruff brute some fifteen years her junior, but with a conspiracy, and that the honest, upright, incorruptible Berthold, aided and abetted by his wife, probably introduced them in the first place. (And they're all in on it, even Matthew, yes, and even Gerald, who has been in almost daily telephone contact with the Hall.) Conversations suddenly stop when I enter a room; they mouth hidden signals behind my back, and exchange meaningful looks when I open my mouth. If I was among strangers I would think I had stale breath. What people will not do to be rid of an awkward sister!

Everything's been planned down to the last detail. Humphry is attending an hotel and catering school owned by a brewery company of which Martha's brother is a director and where apparently he's a star pupil. Matthew's been seeing quite a bit of him and he's been taking him out to his club, to Lords, the races, etc. Pygmalion is being replayed with Matthew in the part of Higgins and Humphry as Liza Doolittle. How funny this would all be if it wasn't so sad.

My dear, you can't imagine the intricacies of the whole plot and the elaborate lengths to which they have gone to keep the whole thing from me. Fetlock has become Byzantium.

In the circumstances I think I may be forgiven for approaching my friend Donegal as soon as I get back to Bor Shachor and, if I may mix metaphors, putting a spoke in Cupid's bow.

I have reservations about the matter for several reasons, not the least of them being what Donegal might want in return. It is my invariable experience that where people insist they want nothing, they expect too much, and Donegal will obviously demand that we ease off from our Save the Seraglio campaign, which is, I think, a reasonable hope, because we may perhaps be acting like Luddites in the matter. I am not sure if we can stop Bor Shachor from taking its rightful place in the twentieth century.

He may also expect us to stop agitating for a Reform synagogue. As you know I am fond of both Nahumi and Gary. They are the best friends I have in Israel, and of course I believe every man should be free to worship what he wants, where he wants, in the way he wants, but Reform synagogues have arisen entirely out of recent European history. They have no natural place in Israel and would be an alien and disruptive import. Once you start extracting what is acceptable in a faith and what isn't, as if it was some great mixed salad, you might as well drop the whole lot. And in any case, do you really want a synagogue, albeit a Reform synagogue, right next door? For even if you have no argument with Reform theology, think of their cars.

I also have the slight feeling that we are both being a little presumptuous. Of course, there is much wrong with Israel in general and Bor Shachor in particular which one would like to put right, but you know even Jesuits acclimatise themselves before setting out to spread the Gospel among the natives. We have been in Bor Shachor under a year and we are trying to turn the place inside out. We haven't seen the country. We took two holidays a year in England, we haven't had one in Israel. We haven't travelled, we've hardly been away for as much as a weekend, and as I look back on our stay it's been almost one ceaseless struggle. I enjoy a fight and so, of course, do you, but would it not be wise to relax for a bit, and to settle in to our new situation before taking up arms? Whatever Israel lacks it will never be short of causes.

I have seen a lot of Gwendoline and have felt closer to her these past few days – especially after I chanced on the family conspiracy – than at any time before. She can be rather attractive, and not only in the dusk with the light behind her. She has fine bone-structure, a handsome neck and glowing sensitive eyes, and if only one could take her aside and suggest that she surrender half her nose, she could be positively beautiful. Which is all the more reason why I am determined to ease her out of her infatuation, and I hope that Donegal may be able to help. If one can no longer depend on one's own family, I think one may be excused for turning to strangers.

All my love,
Your Henry

Dear Celeste,

I can't imagine what's come over you. It is bad enough to say that you have always known me to be weak, pompous and stupid but that it hadn't occurred to you I was a scoundrel; it is infinitely worse to refer to me as such in a letter to Berthold, and, as if that wasn't enough, to ask him to keep an eye on me because you thought I was going mad. I hasten to add that I have not been reading my brother's mail, but in your anxiety to humiliate me you happened to put my letter in his envelope and vice-versa. Or perhaps you intended me to see the letter in the first place.

Yes, it is true that I may have taken Gwendoline's affairs too much to heart and that I may even have allowed it to go to my head, but I always thought that even if all the others were ganged up against me, I could always look to your support for what I was trying to do, and why I was trying to do it, and that you, at least, shared my sense of family. Obviously I was mistaken and I am returning to Israel forthwith.

Henry

Chapter 5

Preservationists All

Dear Gerald,

Thank you for your various cables and the unexpected honour of a long letter. You must have thought I was dying, if not dead.

The reports of my collapse seem to have been embellished in the retelling. What happened simply is that I was taken ill on the plane (I'm a bad flier). The pilot radioed Lud and there was a doctor and ambulance waiting as we arrived, which created a certain amount of commotion, and as you can't blow your nose in Israel without a cameraman capturing the event for eternity, a picture of me being carried down the gangway in a stretcher appeared in several papers, together with at least one report that I was dead, which, by local standards, was hardly an exaggeration.

It all gave poor Celeste a rather nasty shock, especially as it came hard on top of another. A heavy lorry reversed into the Seraglio by 'accident'. Happily, old buildings are rather more formidable than new lorries and the lorry got the worst of the encounter, but it did some damage and unless the owners make some quick repairs, the villa will deteriorate and collapse, which is, of course, exactly what the wreckers want. You can, with a bit of effort, prevent people from killing a building, but you cannot force them to keep it alive.

My indisposition has meant that we've missed Gwendoline's nuptials. She was prepared to postpone them for my sake, but I urged her to proceed as planned and Celeste didn't go because she felt she couldn't leave my side, though I suspect her worries about the Seraglio may also have had something to do with it.

Berthold was good enough to write to me about the wedding in some detail. I am glad that they were able to hold it in the Hall and that the final family event it should have witnessed was Gwendoline's wedding and not Father's funeral. The happy couple have not yet found a suitable site for the sort of hotel they want and once they've found their site the actual building work may take the better part of two hundred years. I've warned them that time round here is no object, and if you complain about the tardiness of this or that individual or department you are told: 'Look we've waited two thousand years to get here, so what's another week?'

The marriage habit is contagious and Matthew is to make an honest woman of his Beatrice and has planned a small wedding in the King David Hotel, Jerusalem. Matthew, of course, has sentimental feelings about the King David for he was blown up there by the Irgun shortly after the war, but we are reasonably hopeful that his wedding will be a less dramatic affair.

I was in hospital for about three weeks, the first of which I was unconscious, the second semi-conscious, and even when I was restored to myself it took me some time to recover my bearings. You were probably too young to remember, but I was called up to the army in the last year of the war (the first one, of course). It was all, I'm afraid, a rather inglorious experience, for I was gassed by my own side, and that during a training exercise, and when I came to I found myself gazing out through the lead-latticed windows of a magnificent Jacobean mansion. You know how one sometimes goes through life feeling that one wasn't born into one's natural place. Waking up in the early hours of a golden summer's day, and gazing out at the lawns, I felt I had been suddenly restored to my *locus naturalis.* It was rather different here. Ever since I received my pension book I have had a dread of losing my private income, being foresaken by my children and finding myself in an old-age home. And this is exactly what I thought had happened now. I sat up and gazed around desperately for Celeste's face. She wasn't there. We had been separated and she would be coming to visit me on Sunday afternoons carrying home-baked fairy cakes, back numbers of *Punch* and photographs of the grandchildren. And I lifted up my voice and wept.

There were six or seven of us in the room, all grey-haired, or white-haired, several of us bearded, one crumpled, bright-eyed little ancient, with a beret on his head and side-curls, was swaying to and fro in his bed, saying prayers in a monotonous chant. One was groaning. Others were arguing or shouting, and I was gradually reassured by the prevailing chaos.

There were, I was told, 'strict' visiting hours, but people came and went as they chose at all times of the day and most hours of the night. The bright-eyed ancient has fourteen children, sixty-six grandchildren and eleven great-grand-children and it sometimes seemed as if they all descended upon him in one clamorous mass. There was a plump man in the bed next to me sitting bolt upright like a Buddha and rarely uttering a word. He spoke a language no one understood which sounded like a croak, but he may have been merely clearing his throat. He never had visitors except some dear elderly ladies in straw hats who made it their business to visit everyone and came around bearing words of comfort and Polo mints. The doctors never saw him either and I have the feel-ing he may have been there as a result of some clerical error.

Most of the patients, to judge from the prevailing aroma, had drainage problems and there was a lean white-haired figure in a dressing gown who shuffled around the place and stopped to chat to various patients. He had some sort of blockage in his bladder and was fitted up with a by-pass which dangled between his legs like a tail and discharged into a plastic bag which he carried in his hand like a briefcase.

'A useful contraption,' he said, 'tells you how you are at a glance.'

He claimed to have been in hospital in four different con-tinents and to have left some part of himself at every stop.

'It's amazing what you can manage without,' he said, 'except that what's left flops around a bit and you've got to move carefully.'

He asked me what I was in for and I said I wasn't sure.

'Didn't the doctors tell you?'

'They don't know either.'

'That's bad, it means they don't want to tell you. Are your bowels regular?'

'Fairly regular.'

'Any bleeding?'

'I don't think so.'

'And is the end-product runny or solid?'

'I don't know, I don't keep an eye on these things.'

'You should at your age. Got any pains?'

He carried a small torch with him and offered to look up my anus. He had had so much contact with medicine and hospitals that I think he regarded himself as a common law doctor.

The only sensation I could complain of was a slight dizziness and I couldn't understand what I was doing in hospital till I tried to get on my feet and found that they sank under me, an odd feeling, as if they were turning to water. I then moved about supported by two buxom nurses, an experience, I may tell you, which is no incentive to recover the use of your legs. Celeste came to see me two or three times a week and she brought me half a library, but I found I couldn't concentrate on anything except what was happening about me in the ward, and in particular the nurses, brisk, dark, darting creatures, whose every movement I followed with a hunger that was faintly reassuring. Where there's lust there's life.

A pair of Rabbis came to visit me. I had been asleep and woke to find these two pale-faced, bearded figures sitting on either side of me. They reminded me at once of the pair who came to lay out poor Father and say prayers for his departed soul and I thought that my time had come and I was immediately overwhelmed with a great pang of regret for things I had left unfinished, the new life upon which Celeste and I had only just embarked and which we had yet to live, all accompanied by groans from the beds about me. I was in purgatory, it seemed. But then the smell of cooking wafted in from the kitchen and I felt as if my soul was wafting back into my body. I sat up in bed, alive, and it has occurred to me that what we talk of as souls may be no more than chicken-soup vapour.

I confounded the doctors and if they don't know what caused my collapse they don't know what cured me. It may have been merely the sight of the nurses, though what probably jostled me into recovery was the sudden realisation that I wasn't in Britain and wasn't insured and that I was paying for my bed. I phoned Celeste to collect me without delay, but when she arrived I found that I could not be discharged without a receipt from the cashier.

'Whatever for?'

'To show that you have paid the bill.'

'But I haven't received a bill.'

'You'll get one from the cashier.'

Which I did, but then discovered that I didn't have my cheque book.

'You'll have it in the post,' I said airily, but they didn't trust me, or perhaps they didn't trust the post, and they more or less insisted that I stay on as a deposit while Celeste went back for my cheque book. An odd system, don't you think? I'm surprised the place isn't full of abandoned relatives. Anyway, I was all dressed and packed and ready to go, and was unwilling to go back to my bed (which was by then in any case already occupied by another patient) and so I went to a downstairs toilet, climbed through the window onto Celeste's shoulders and away we went. An exhilarating experience. I recommend Israel to you if only for the scope it provides for such small adventures.

I take it, by the way, that you've heard William's had a daughter, the first female in the family and we were so delighted with the news that even Celeste allowed something like a smile to invade her face. She is a dear, compassionate creature, my good wife, but smiles aren't her forté. That brings the number of our grandchildren up to half a dozen, a nice round number, and Rodney has still to do his bit – if he ever gets round to doing it, which is beginning to seem doubtful. Get your daughters married, dear boy, for there's no better compensation for the onset of years than grandchildren.

Yours,

Henry

My dear William,

Your mother brought me the news while I was still in hospital and I thought of writing to you straight away, but so many happy thoughts rushed in upon me that she suggested I calm down before putting pen to paper.

But first an apology. Of course I should have called to see you when I was in London, and I would certainly have done so had I known Helene was in hospital, but I'm afraid that the illness which was to overcome me in Israel was already burgeoning and I was not myself. I didn't call Stanley either, or Rodney (though I'm not really sure where he is), and as a matter of fact I was only in town for a matter of days and had a lot to see to, for my affairs are in disorder and the fact that poor Grosskopf has dropped dead didn't help things either. I am relieved to hear that the birth passed off without complication and that dear Helene is much better. And how is the child? Does she take after her mother?

Boys are everything in Jewish life but it is nice to have a girl for a change. We are a rather masculine family. Father had four sons and a daughter, and we only had sons, so you can imagine with what joy your mother and I have greeted the birth of a grand-daughter. No doubt you and Helene will have chosen a name by now, but if not, I thought you might wish to call her after your dear grandmother. I know that Gladys is not a fashionable name nowadays, but these things go in cycles and by the time the child grows to maturity it could well be in fashion again. Gerald intended, or said he intended, to call his daughters after her, but he forgot each time, and poor mother was the sort of person about whom one always did. She was such a sweet, timid, self-effacing soul and I feel one should do something to keep her memory alive, don't you? But that is only a suggestion. Don't, for heaven's sake, let me interfere with your choice.

Give my love to la belle Helene and to dear Jason and Jeremy. How have they taken the advent of a baby sister? Wouldn't it be nice if they could write to me about it?

Your loving father,
Henry

Dear Berthold,

Thank you for your long letter which, as you can imagine, I read with avid interest. One need only drop dead, or appear to be dropping dead, to discover what friends one has. I was overwhelmed with letters and messages, even Gerald wrote to me, at *length*, and by *hand*.

I was in hospital for about three weeks and returned restored in health though depleted in money. Those of us who have grown to maturity on the dear old National Health (with the added underpinning of BUPA), don't know what it is to be ill abroad, but it could be worse for, as Gerald pointed out, a three-weeks' stay in an American hospital could have ruined me for life and death. Prices are also rising by the day, which means that we are beginning to eat into our capital and at this rate I fear we may soon eat our way out of it and I am more eager than ever to find a new source of income. Bassetts, as you know, have not been too helpful, and Parkinsons, to whom I have written since, have not even replied. I suppose they are afraid to give a franchise in Israel for fear of the Arab boycott.

In the meantime we have had to cut down on a few of our old indulgences. We no longer eat imported breakfast cereals (I have worked out that English sugar puffs work out at about a *grusch* a puff) and we make do with the local products which look and taste like (and probably are) a poultry food, but which are comparatively inexpensive. And it's no more Earl Grey tea (we still have a caddy left, but use it only on the Sabbath and state occasions). My bowels are no longer kept in motion by All Bran, it's goodbye to Marmite, and Skippers sardines and Hellman's mayonnaise and Oxford marmalade, and patum pepperium, and anchovies, and Andrew's Liver Salts and Bourn-Vita. The last in particular was a wrench, but gradually I have accommodated myself to cocoa instead and it is really amazing what one can manage without if one has to. Celeste, certainly, seems impervious to privation or indeed to anything except the battle for the Seraglio which is about to enter a crucial phase. I must have told you there was an attempt to sabotage the building – a heavy lorry went into it at a point where it forms part of the surrounding wall, but the damage was not as heavy as she at first feared, and the special party she organised to carry out emergency repairs under the cover of darkness did not have to go into action. On the other hand the discovery of the skeleton did not delay things for as long as she had hoped. The bones were found, on examination, to be of recent origin (they were in fact found to belong to a local medical student, and how they got there is a mystery), and although others were discovered nearby they were not human so that even the Rabbis are satisfied that the area was not the site of a Jewish cemetery and the way is now clear for the wreckers. Or at least so Nahumi thinks, and so does Michaeli, but Celeste does not give up so easily, and she has found help from a new source, namely Gwendoline, who has only just settled in, but is already a power in the place.

You should have been here when she and Humphry descended on Bor Shachor – it was like the arrival of the Queen of Sheba. They docked at Ashdod where they were received by a clamorous concourse of over three hundred relatives (some of them bearing their portraits aloft as if they were icons) who showered them with rice and almonds and streamers and it took the entire corpus of the port police to clear a way. On the approaches to Bor Shachor they were greeted by police outriders and escorted into town. When they pulled into the piazza half the town turned out to receive them, kiss them, shake their hands, festoon them with flowers, clap, shout, cheer. The crowds were so dense that the couple had to complete the last part of their royal progress on foot and in the ensuing commotion some of their luggage and two of their car tyres were stolen, which spoilt things a bit.

The press and television were of course on hand, and Gwendoline has been described in several papers as a member of one of the oldest and best-known Jewish families in England. I must say she photographs well and her height makes her look regal. Humphry photographs rather less well, especially in a broad-brimmed panama hat. He, one gathers from press reports, is descended from a succession of Rabbis and saints, and almost everyone regards their marriage as a symbolic union of East and West, though here and there the treatment was a little more romantic and in some papers their story was made to read like an updated account of the princess and the swine-herd.

I don't know who stage-managed the whole festival. I suspect it was Celeste. She has found the pair accommodation next door to us in Gary's villa (his plan for a Reform synagogue has had to be shelved for the time being), and has already enrolled Gwendoline as Vice-President of the Save Bor Shachor campaign and I have no doubt that she will be a great asset, for she and her husband comprise the beginnings of a local gentry, with Humphry in the improbable role of squire.

Whatever impediments stood in the way of Matthew's marriage have been cleared up and the wedding is to take place in Jerusalem in a couple of weeks. Any chance of you and Martha being here for it? It is to be a quiet wedding, but they don't even have quiet funerals round here and it promises to be a fairly colourful affair. Besides, it would be nice to see you. Our guest room is, of course, at your disposal.

I am surprised you haven't received a single serious bid for the Hall. I would have thought with all those companies moving out of London and into the countryside some might be happy to acquire a place like the Hall for their HQ. Or, failing that, have you thought of converting it into a hotel? It could make a sound investment. I know it is a little remote (which is why Father built it where he did), but everybody has cars these days and it is well within a two-hour drive of London and under an hour from Chelmsford. The thought of the dear old Hall going out of the family's hands is rather sad, the thought of it being converted into an hotel – with all the squalid things which go on in such places – is even sadder, but I understand your quandary.

Yours ever,
Henry

Dear Berthold,

A pity you and Martha couldn't attend the wedding. It was a happy little affair, or at least it was meant to be little.

Some fifty people were invited, but over a hundred turned up. Invitations tend to be slightly irrelevant here for if people aren't invited they come to show that they take no umbrage. We once attended a wedding at Bor Shachor and most of the food and drink had vanished by the time we arrived and we thought we must have come very late, but the actual wedding ceremony hadn't even started. Matthew's was a rather more decorous affair – though even there the buffet was devoured long before the last guests were on the scene, and new supplies were hurriedly brought in.

Nicky had wanted a visiting American Reform Rabbi to perform the ceremony, but that might have created an international incident, for Reform clergy are not recognised as Rabbis in Israel, which did not worry Matthew at all, but I put it to him that, as the family were always among the pillars of Anglo-Jewish Orthodoxy and, moreover, seeing he was finally taking the trouble of getting married, he might as well do it properly and have it kosher.

'But I've never had anything to do with Rabbis,' he protested.

'I'll find you one,' I said, and called on my friend, Mittwoch, to invite him to perform the ceremony. He was overwhelmed.

'Thank God, a *simcha.* I've been burying people all week.' He poured me a glass of brandy and we both drank a hearty *le'chaym.*

'Who is it? A child? A grandchild? A niece?'

'My brother,' I said. At which his brandy went down the wrong way and he coughed and spluttered and struggled with a purple face to regain his voice.

'You mean the old man?'

'Matthew.'

'He, who, him – Mr Hoch, I am not hearing to low gossip, I am not hearing even to high gossip, but Bor Shachor is a little place, and if someone does dirty work, everybody hears it – everybody hears it even if they don't do it, so if they do do it, even I hear it.'

'Are you referring to my brother's affair with Mrs Gittleson?'

'I am not saying anything.'

'Then what are you saying?'

'It wasn't nice.'

'I agree, but what could I do? He's beyond the age of consent, to be honest I thought he was beyond the age of mischief, but in any case he now wants to make an honest woman out of her.'

'An honest woman?'

'Yes.'

'Out of her?'

'Yes.'

'A married woman with two children.'

'But she's divorced now.'

'She not divorced then, then she was a dishonest woman.' He found the whole situation too delicate to cope with in English and he reverted to Hebrew and he was trying to tell me that as Nicky and Matthew had lived together while she was still technically a married woman, they could not be married in Jewish law.

'She is forbidden to her husband and her boyfriend.'

'Is that the law?'

'It is from Heaven.'

'I didn't know that.'

'You didn't ask – he didn't ask. Nobody asks, they just do. Sodom was a city of innocents compared to Bor Shachor.'

I then turned to Rabbi Selah (without, of course, mentioning my encounter with Mittwoch). He too had heard the gossip, but the first thing he asked was: 'How old is your brother?'

'Seventy-four.'

'He is an old man.'

'He will be seventy-five in another month or two,' I said and suggested that the whole idea of a man of Matthew's age committing adultery was absurd. He and Nicky had lived together for companionship, which may have been an imprudent thing to do, but it was hardly the squalid affair people suggested.

'He is too old?'

'Far too old.'

'He cannot have children?'

'Have you met my brother?'

'Yes.'

'Does he look as if he can have children?'

'You cannot tell from the face.'

'He cannot have children,' I said categorically, which I suppose is a lie.

'Well,' said the Rabbi, 'if he cannot have children, he cannot marry.'

'Is that the law?'

'It is from Heaven.'

I finally found a young Rabbi who asked no questions and to whom I told no lies. He could have been Matthew's grandson, but addressed the pair as if they were a young couple on the threshold of life, and as the audience was large and distinguished he continued till the guests had drifted away from the *chupah* and on to the tables.

Matthew was in a morning coat and grey topper and looked as if he had just come out of the Royal Enclosure at Ascot, and Nicky looked delectable in a canary-coloured suit and white blouse, with a little bit of yellow netting in lieu of a hat, and when she appeared by his side the looks of envy he received were almost audible, and it was not difficult to catch muttered asides like :

'What does a little thing like her see in an old buck like him?' Or, 'She's even got money.' To think that our dear brother, for so long the source of family pride and then of consternation, should in his old age have become a source of envy.

While the Rabbi was still in full spate, Gerald appeared from nowhere, gave Matthew a congratulatory thump on the back, kissed the bride, apologised to the public and fled. I am not sure if he was there by chance or had flown in specially for the occasion.

It was a mixed gathering. A lot of kissing and not a few kissable Americans who rushed around with jangling bangles falling upon each other like actresses, and tall, slow-moving, elderly ex-colonial types with loud Poona voices. 'Matthew, dear boy, never knew you were still alive, let alone lively enough to take a wife.' And weaving among them was a collection of lithe dusky figures who were not invited, but who go wherever Humphry goes. Cousins, I suppose. Gwendoline looks splendid. She always had a certain stateliness to her, but the final effect, because of her height and temperament was rather bleak and glacial. I wouldn't say that she radiates sunshine even now, but she does give the distinct impression that there is blood flowing in her veins, and precious blood at that. Those of us who prognosticated that her marriage would be a disaster have so far been proved wrong. Long may we continue to stand contradicted.

Yours ever,
Henry

Dear Gerald,

You may remember I suggested to you half-humorously that you might be interested in buying the Hall to keep it in the family, and you replied that if you went in for a country seat you would look for something Tudor or Plantagenet. The Hall, to be sure, is neither of these things, but it was our home, and I think we would all be sorry to see it demolished, which is what may happen. It has now been on the market for over six months and has not attracted as much as a serious inquiry, let alone a bid. I put it to Berthold that he might wish to convert it into a hotel, and he replied that while he would be perfectly happy to let others do so, he is too old to branch out in a new line of business, nor, as he put it, is the catering trade quite his scene. On the other hand he has moved all his personal effects to his London home and is keeping a skeleton staff to defend the place from vandals and/or squatters, and even skeleton staffs are hard to find, harder to keep, troublesome and expensive, and it costs a small fortune to keep the building heated and in repair.

Now you mentioned when last I saw you that you were about to open a London office. Many companies which have had offices in London for many years are finding it so expensive, and debilitating, that they are moving out into the country. Wouldn't you care to do the same? The Hall, as you know, is only about an hour and a half's drive from London (if you avoid the rush hours and Bank Holiday traffic). You would have a spacious edifice in a beautiful setting at a fraction of the London price, and although it is difficult to keep domestic staff in the area, it should be not at all difficult to attract secretarial and administrative staff for thousands of Londoners are scratching around for an opportunity to get out to the countryside. Finally, the Hall is hardly more than forty minutes drive from Cambridge. You would be within easy reach of your daughter and she of you (you could adapt three or four rooms for your own personal use), and, above all, you would be keeping the family home in the family. Don't you think it's a brilliant idea?

Yours,
Henry

Dear Berthold,

I have written to Gerald suggesting that he might wish to acquire the Hall, but his response – in a three-word cable – has been less than enthusiastic. Gwendoline will have written to you about her own feelings on the matter. She would be sorry to see the Hall die, but does not feel that anyone need strive officiously to keep it alive – so there we are.

Gwendoline has, with the help of Celeste, found a site for the hotel, or rather a building which is to be converted into an hotel – and it is to be none other than the Seraglio, provided, of course, that it can be saved from the wreckers, and Gwendoline's plans may well save it.

She had been thinking in terms of a pocket Hilton of glass and concrete, but now that Celeste has won her over to the Seraglio, she is planning to convert it into an eighteenth-century-style English coaching inn. She is to call it the Fox and Hounds, which should tell you everything, and certainly as far as size is concerned, the Seraglio with its twenty rooms, outhouses and large cobbled courtyard is just about right. She has even induced an English brewer – Martha's brother, in fact – to express an interest in the place. I had no idea that she was, apart from anything else, a skilled businesswoman, did you? I cannot quite see Humphry in the role of mine host, but I might be as wrong about him as I have been about too many other things. His English, by the way, has improved immensely.

In the meantime, however, the Seraglio is not yet hers and the actual plans for the building are far from clear.

Celeste met the Minister of Housing at some sort of gathering and she raised the matter with him, and he asked her to come and see him at the Ministry, but by then there had been a Government reshuffle and the new Minister knew little of Celeste and that little he didn't much care for and he told her that Israel was not England, that it was chock-full of history and that if it was to abandon itself to the preservation game it would be doing nothing else.

Humphry undertook to organise a mass petition, but with the same fatal aptitude for excess enthusiasm that he has always shown in the past, and within a matter of weeks amassed no less than fifty thousand signatures against the demolition of the Seraglio, an impressive total, one might think, especially as Bor Shachor has a population of about forty thousand of whom at least ten thousand are illiterate.

In the meantime, we have complied with the court order and are desisting from formal obstruction, and have resorted instead to the informal sort. Cars and lorries keep breaking down at certain strategic points around the Seraglio. At other times I might bring out a table and chairs and have a hand of bridge in the street. It is all a bit of a strain, for we have to use western immigrants (the police have scant respect for orientals) and there aren't so many of us about, but we have also won the support of a nearby kibbutz, Givat Schmertz, which is of immense help for kibbutznicks are even more sacrosanct than Anglo-Saxons.

All these are, of course, temporary steps, but they have helped to demoralise the opposition and there seems to have been no attempt to get at the site either by vehicles or workmen, or perhaps everybody is too preoccupied with the coming elections to have a mind for anything else.

We have hitherto been a loose, ad-hoc group of individuals interested in preserving the Seraglio, but there are numerous other things which we want to have put right and a few days

ago we had a large public meeting to establish the Bor Shachor
society, and we got off to a good start for the place was packed
with a crowd of over four hundred.

The size of the gathering is slightly misleading, for public
meetings round here are a form of entertainment in their own
right, and whatever the occasion one can depend on at least
a hundred passers-by dropping in from the street to see what,
if anything, is happening. Others were Humphry's relatives
who, as I mentioned earlier, follow him as if he was the Pied
Piper. Others still, I suppose, wanted a closer look at Gwendoline, and to shake hands with her, in case any part of her
legendary wealth should rub off, but I would say that about
a third of the audience was seriously interested in what we were
trying to do, which gives us a good solid base for our opera-
tions.

Our basic aim is to make Bor Shachor a better place to
live in. We were opposed to tower blocks in general and called
for the preservation not only of the Seraglio but for the entire
remnant of old Quolboyeh. We also wanted the swimming
pool to be completed for public use and demanded that the
local park, which was hardly more than a rubbish dump and
trysting place for stray cats and libidinous couples, be properly
seeded, planted and policed. And finally, we wanted all religious
denominations in the town to enjoy, and to be seen to enjoy,
complete freedom of worship.

This last point which was of course put in on behalf of
Gary and his Reform group, caused some controversy, because
most people thought there was complete freedom of worship
in the town, and others felt that it had nothing to do with our
basic aim, but Celeste insisted that there was more to a social
environment than buildings, swimming pools and parks; there
had to be understanding and fairness, and after some argument
she had her way.

Among all this commotion she has still found time to show
Gwendoline round the shops and to teach her how to haggle,
to which she took very easily and if she ever gets back to
London, you'll find her haggling in Harrods.

For much of my life I used to be introduced as my father's
son, then as Celeste's husband. Now I am introduced as

Gwendoline's brother or as Humphry's brother-in-law. There's fame for you.

Yours ever,
Henry

Dear Mr Grosskopf,

Thank you for your letter.

I am sorry for leaving my affairs in such disorder, but I felt fairly disordered myself and I was afraid that if I remained in England another day, I might expire. As it was I nearly expired by the time I reached Israel, though you will be glad to hear that I have since made a good recovery.

I appreciate your advice about my share portfolio. Everyone keeps urging me to cut my losses, but my own feeling is that my holding, having fallen this far, can only rise, and my natural inclination is to do nothing unless there are unanswerable grounds for doing something, which there aren't in this case. There are shares which one holds on to as an act of faith rather than as an investment, but I am not sure what you mean by 'presumably your holding in the House of Hoch is not governed by market considerations?' Are you saying that if it was, you would advise me to sell?

Perhaps you might be good enough to enlarge on this matter.

Yours sincerely,
Henry Hoch

Dear Berthold,

Donegal has been threatening us with an invitation to his home ever since I got to know him, which is over six months ago, and I hadn't felt that our relationship had ever developed to the point where the invitation would be served. Moreover, I couldn't quite see him having a normal home life, with a wife and children. One gets the feeling that he lives on politics and that he goes to sleep at night on a mattress under his desk (if not in a drawer in his desk), but he in fact has a nice home with a nice wife, a portly little woman (though bigger than him), with a sweet face who didn't open her mouth for the entire evening; he made up for her. There were no other guests and the fare consisted of a variety of nuts and various local spirits (which make up in potency what they lack in finesse), plus half a bottle of something called Paddy, an Irish whiskey which I had never heard of; and which he poured out drop by drop as if he was parting with his own blood, which in a sense he was. It was his last lingering taste of Ireland, he said, and once it was gone he would be leaving Ireland behind him for good.

He had asked us round because, as he put it, he wanted to appeal to the Jew in us. Most Jews who came to Israel from places like Britain and America, he said, came there for religious reasons, because Israel was the one place where they could lead a full Jewish life.

'There was nothing to stop us leading a full Jewish life in Isleworth,' interjected Celeste.

'Yes, yes, but here in Israel when it's Shabbat, you know it's Shabbat; when it's Yom Tov you know it's Yom Tov – you feel it in the air, but in other ways it isn't quite the holy place people like to think it is. You see the trouble with us God-fearing people is that we leave too much to the Almighty and do too little ourselves. That's how it was with Palestine. Who were the Zionist pioneers? Not us. While we prayed for the return to Zion, young socialists came out and built it and, by the time we arrived, they were in charge of everything that counts, as they deserved to be, and as they still are, but things are beginning to move our way. "There's a tide in the affairs of men, which grasped . . ." you know what I mean.'

We did.

'Well, it has come here in Bor Shachor. There's an election due in a few months, and for the first time the Holy Alliance has the chance to grasp power, not as a member of a coalition, but in its own right. It could make Bor Shachor a centre of living Judaism. Did you know that the Ark of the Covenant stopped here in the days of the Judges?'

'No, I didn't.'

'That's just one of the discoveries our archaeologists have made and that there was a Temple of sorts here long before

Solomon was ever born. They discovered the foundation only two days ago, but I hope they'll be open to the public by the end of the month, and if we play our cards right and win the next election Bor Shachor could revert to its ancient role as a holy city. It would become a place of learning and pilgrimage. We would rebuild our main synagogue on the lines of the Temple. People would come here from the world over to withdraw from the strains and stresses of mortal life, and dwell upon the eternities.'

'Where do we come in?' asked Celeste.

'The Seraglio business. I think you must have discovered by now that your opposition to the scheme is futile. Don't misunderstand me. I appreciate what you're trying to do – sure, I'm half tempted to join you myself – but if Bor Shachor is to acquire what the estate agents back home used to call a desirable area, it has to be on the escarpment, well away from the industrial zone and the immigrant housing. The whole scheme is our child. I mean the Holy Alliance's. I found the investors' company is part of the Alliance.'

'You mean,' said Celeste, slightly aghast, 'that the Holy Alliance is in business?'

'Everything and everybody here is in business. It's the only way of staying alive. Business means jobs, influence, power. Where do you think the Workers' League would be without their banks and insurance companies and their public contracting company? We already have the towers on the drawing boards, and in glorious Technicolor on the billboards. That sort of thing impresses nobody any more, for the whole country is awash with blueprints, but once we have men actually on the job – it could mean thousands of votes. There is heavy unemployment in the area. We had a textile plant closing down only last month and there are hundreds of people idle. Every man you offer a job could have seven or eight dependants, to say nothing of more remote relatives. A start now would give jobs now and hold out the hope of other jobs in the near future.'

'Everybody is clamouring for a swimming pool,' said Celeste. 'Why don't you finish it and open it to the public? It could also mean work.'

'So would a brothel. Can you imagine what a swimming pool would do to a place like Bor Shachor? It would cause no end of mischief.'

'What do you mean?'

'This is what I mean. If we did have a pool, we would of course have it segregated, but in no time people would be clamouring for mixed bathing, and even if they weren't clamouring for it you couldn't prevent it because, given the way young people look and dress these days, you can't always tell who's what until they're stripped down and in the water and of course it's too late by then.'

'We have mixed bathing in Isleworth,' I said, 'but I've read no reports of aquatic orgies.'

'Sure, and there's mixed bathing in Cork, but Bor Shachor isn't Isleworth or even Cork, and there's no knowing what they could get up to once you brought them together half naked. Look, I'm no prude. I take my family for a weekly swim to a nearby kibbutz and I wouldn't dream of stopping anyone else from doing the same, but what you can do as an individual you can't do as a municipality. And even if we in Bor Shachor were tempted to go ahead with the swimming pool, the party as a whole is against it. Can you imagine what would happen if word got around that the Holy Alliance favoured mixed bathing?'

'They'd get the floating vote,' I ventured, but he was not amused.

'We'd be finished. There are wild men on our right, the fuzzy wuzzies, waiting to show we've no principles and are ready to sell out to the nearest bidder. No, my dear, the swimming pool is out, but if you will drop your opposition to the tower blocks I can promise you a Bor Shachor in which it will be a pleasure to live and a privilege to die. I know I've spoken about Bor Shachor as a holy city, but we could also do with a few people with money, besides your good selves, and the towers would bring them. It would also help your sister. She wants to build a hotel – bless her – and of course we are offering her every facility, even if her plans are on the humble side, but you know hotels depend on local custom – a wedding, a Barmitzvah, a New Year's eve party, a Rotary luncheon, people celebrating some private anniversary, or taking their friends out to a meal – '

'Or having a dirty weekend?' I suggested.

'What people do in the privacy of their own room is their business, but in any case who is there in Bor Shachor who can afford a decent coffee in a clean cup, never mind a whole weekend? Money begets money. Frankly, Bor Shachor isn't ready for her hotel yet, but it will be once the towers are up. It'll be the Claridge's of the place. But that's all beside the point, what I wanted to ask you is – do you regard yourselves as religious Jews, or not?'

'We're Jews,' said Celeste, 'we don't go in for prefixes.'

'But don't you want the place to have a Jewish feel? Wouldn't it be nice if you went out on a Friday night and found everything tranquil and silent, with young people at home, in the bosom of their family, celebrating the Sabbath, instead of gathered together in some low-class café listening to a juke-box?'

'I dare say I would, but if young people prefer juke-boxes to the bosom of their family, who can stop them?'

'We could close down the cafés for a start, at least on Friday night. We would create a different sort of atmosphere and if the atmosphere was different we'd attract a different type of resident. The sacred drives out the profane. I'm not such a saint myself, but there's one thing about the Orthodox, they're home-loving, they're peace-loving, they've got self-discipline. There's no problem of juvenile delinquency. You don't have to send truant catchers round to whip them into school, they're hard-working. Once an area becomes religious, you can halve the size of your police-force. You sometimes have to double the number of your dustmen, but on balance I'd rather have more dustmen than policemen. Moreover – partly because of the attention which you and your dear sister-in-law have brought to the place – people have their eyes on Bor Shachor, and if we could show them a religious-controlled council, which had proper reverence for the past, but which still had an eye to the future – '

'That's where the tower blocks come in.'

'They're part of it.'

'Can you think of no better symbol of progress?'

'What do you want, sex-shops? The whole of Israel is watching us and if we could show them an example of a religious municipality that works, it would give new heart and confidence to the Holy Alliance in the whole country. You'd be giving God a chance in his own kingdom. Israel isn't England. There, people revere religion even if they don't believe in it, so that you can still have an established church in a pagan country. You wouldn't get that here. The non-religious are anti-religious. If religion, tradition, the past, mean anything at all to you, you've got to take the side of the Holy Alliance. There's my final message : if you're not with us, you're against us.'

I'm afraid we shall be against him.

Yours ever,
Henry

Dear Berthold,

Please forgive me for raising a subject on which you have been reticent, which, indeed, you have not mentioned at all, which I would not have mentioned either but for the fact that we read the English papers here (or at least the papers that count) and we could not help noticing the prominence given to your affairs, and some of the reports have even been picked up in the Hebrew press (with the aside that 'Mr Berthold Hoch, the Chairman of the Company, is a brother-in-law of Mrs Celeste Hoch). I hasten to add that none of the reports suggest anything to your discredit and not a few pay tribute to your standing as a symbol of that probity which has almost lapsed from business life, but they all dwell rather lugubriously on your difficulties, and they are flapping around like vultures waiting for the kill. The shares, of course, have been in decline for the past year or two, but it was only when they began plummeting last week that Gwendoline and I realised that something had gone seriously wrong and that, bad as the news was, there was worse to come.

Neither Gwendoline nor I approached you on the matter because we didn't want to add to your troubles, but what troubles us is that you gave no hint that you were experiencing any difficulties beyond those common to British business life (which in all conscience are difficult enough). In fact, you didn't mention the company at all, which I should have seen as a warning of sorts. I am aware that you are not the sort of man who likes to share his troubles, but surely as your brother and sister we had some right to know. We only hope that your silence on the matter did not arise out of the fear that either Gwendoline or I would dispose of our shares at the first hint of trouble. You may feel assured that we shall hold on to them to the last. I am not sure if one can say the same for Gerald, who has a genius for getting out while the going is good. My holding, as you know, is not large, so it will hardly affect me one way or the other, and although Gwendoline's is considerable, she said she'd discounted it years ago. The banks, I see, are organising some sort of salvage operation, which presumably means that all is lost, at least as far as the ordinary shareholders are concerned, but that in a sense is the minor part of it all. What pains me is the thought that the House of Hoch, seventy years old this year, is to be no more. Can they save nothing from the wreck – not even the name?

Our most immediate concern is, of course, about you. One need hardly add that you have nothing to reproach yourself with, except the fact that you handed over control to your children before they had the sagacity and the experience to exercise it. They were obviously eager not to be thought of merely as the progeny of a rich father and a very rich grand-father, and sought to establish themselves as merchant adventurers in their own right, but were, I'm afraid, rather more adventurers than merchants. They bought too widely and expanded too fast. There is more to being a businessman than sniffing out bargains and padding out the balance sheets with meaningless takeovers. You will recall the dramatic period three years ago when the shares almost doubled in the course of a month. 'I don't like it,' I said to Celeste at the time, 'thank God the boys are out of the company and in the professions.' Indeed, you were more than a little troubled yourself and I said why don't you go in and bang their heads together and you said : 'One either resigns one's responsibility and gives people a free hand, or one doesn't. I did.' We see the consequences now.

I suppose we should be grateful that we were prevented by law from investing any part of the family trust in equities, so you will not be left penniless, but these things are relative and by the age of seventy-nine (or is it eighty?) one has acquired a way of life which is not easy to change over night. And then, of course, there are all your commitments which, knowing you, you will continue to honour, though frankly if I were in your position I would claim an honourable discharge.

The news that you failed to get planning permission to demolish the Hall and erect a housing estate does not surprise me at all, and I take it from your letter that you did not vest much hope in your scheme either. England isn't Israel and one can't cover up a hole in the ground without bringing out the Friends of the Holes in the Ground in protest. Isn't there supposed to be a housing shortage in the country? On what grounds did they reject your plans? Presumably you'll appeal, in the meantime can I ask you for a full and candid account of your position?

> Yours ever,
> Henry

Dear Gerald,

I hesitate to take up your time, but presumably you must know that Berthold is in difficulties and that although trading in his shares has not been suspended, nobody is willing to buy them and everyone is eager to sell them. I do not claim to be an expert in these things, but it has occurred to me that if someone of your standing in the business world was to express an interest in the company, wouldn't that push the shares up a little, and once they began creeping upwards wouldn't that encourage the timid folk to come out from behind their portfolios and start buying, which would send them up further, which would . . . etc? It has always seemed that dabbling in shares is like flying a kite. If one can just get enough breeze under the flaps to get it off the ground it will shoot up to the sky. I am not, of course, so sanguine as to think that anyone who acquired their shares more than two years ago would ever get their money back, but I am pained to see – as I am sure you must be – the famed House of Hoch brought low (if you will forgive the pun). I am aware that, unlike the rest of us, you owe your success to your own efforts, but it could not have been a disadvantage, even in New York, to have been known as the son of Solomon Hoch and I think you owe it to the memory of Father to try to keep the firm alive, even if plain commercial considerations should dictate otherwise, and, if it's too late for that, the name at least should be saved and perpetuated.

Yours,
Henry

Dear Berthold,

I had a curious visit from a journalist the other day. The young man wanted to write a piece about our family and I was sufficiently flattered to be more than usually expansive. He asked me a great deal about Father, about you, about Matthew, and Gwendoline too (I asked him why he didn't interview her in person, but he said her Hebrew wasn't good enough, but mine isn't that much better, and in any case he had a fairly reasonable command of English and he clearly alighted on me because he had been told – I don't know by whom – that I was the family twit).

He wanted to know if I had a picture of the Hall, which by chance I did and I'm afraid in my enthusiasm I may have given him the impression that in the league of stately homes it stood somewhere between Chatsworth and Woburn Abbey. I did not, of course, suggest that it was as old as them (or as large), but I did say, that it was a gem of late Edwardian architecture, that its grand staircase and gallery were the particular objects of admiration, and that it contained priceless glass and timber from an earlier manor which had stood on the same site.

Why then, he asked, was it to be demolished – which is where I should have smelled a rat. 'Oh, no,' I continued innocently, 'there are no plans to demolish it. It might be converted to more modern use, because people don't have the money or the servants to run such places as private homes any more, but the building itself, he could be sure, would remain intact. I would hardly be exerting myself to save a building in Bor Shachor and have my own birthplace demolished.'

These words appeared a few days later under a huge picture of the Hall (with a photo of me inset), with the further declaration – which I did *not* make – that 'this building is forever' (well, I did call it a gem, and a gem is a sort of diamond). It is always a little embarrassing to be confronted with one's enthusiasms at an early hour of the morning. What made it worse was the arrival of your letter informing me that you had after all received planning permission to demolish the Hall and build a housing estate in its place – which is, of course, good news. But presumably the paper had received some advance information and the interview was arranged to embarrass Celeste, as indeed it has done. But I must say she took it rather well, too well for my liking, and I said to her, aren't you cross with me? And she said: 'There's no point in being cross with you, Henry, you are what you are, and I've learned to live with it. Besides, I'm happy for Berthold.'

Yesterday she was surrounded by reporters who asked the obvious question, how could she presume to lead a preservation movement in Bor Shachor if her own ancestral home was being demolished? She replied at once that it was not *her* home, but her husband's. She was not at all sure that it was being demolished and even if it was she did not mix in my affairs and I did not mix in hers. It made me a little bit uneasy to read it, for she sounded a little like a starlet denying rumours of marriage. 'We're only friends', she might have added.

Rodney was to have come out to join us, but has as yet failed to materialise. Have you seen anything of him?

When is the demolition to begin? Do you think I could ask you to save me a small memento from the wreckage? Say, one of the fireplaces. Presumably Gwendoline has written to you about saving some of the timbers for her (she wants them for the Fox and Hounds). Difficult to think of Fetlock without the Hall.

Yours ever,
Henry

Dear Berthold,

What you say is incredible. Who could possibly want to save the Hall? It's the sort of building you have to be born in to cherish. It's a hotch-potch of a place and if it has any distinction or character it arises out of the eccentricities of Father's taste. It is not, by English definitions at least, an old building. It is in an obscure, unvisited and unknown part of the county. The only edifice with any antiquity or charm in the village is the Fox and Hounds, and they've messed about with that. We may have sentimental feelings about the Hall; our children have none. So who would want to save it?

Yours ever,

Henry

Dear Rodney,

Your mother and I were wondering why you hadn't turned up in Bor Shachor as arranged. Now we know.

To say, as you have done, that you are doing in Fetlock what we are trying to do in Bor Shachor is, I'm afraid, rather simplifying the situation. I enclose a picture of the Seraglio. Compare it with what you remember of the Hall and see if they may be spoken of in the same breath. What is perhaps more to the point, England is full of stately homes, unstately homes, olde towns, olde villages, old buildings, castles, churches. Israel too is full of antiquities, but mostly underground, and as far as Bor Shachor is concerned the Seraglio and the handful of villas on either side are the only buildings of distinction in the entire region. There is also a tendency here – which there isn't in England – to demolish first and ask questions afterwards, which we are trying to check otherwise the country will become a wilderness of concrete and glass. Moreover, your aunt Gwendoline, who speaks so highly of you, has plans to convert the Seraglio into an eighteenth-century-style English coaching inn. There is no way of putting the Hall to any economic use and during the many months it was on the market it did not attract one serious bid. If it is readily vendible now it is only because Berthold has at long last received permission to demolish it. As a building it is an encumbrance, as a site it is invaluable.

All that having been said I will admit that for all my reservations about the appearance of the Hall, I have a certain sentimental attachment to it, and it would be nice to see it preserved, and even nicer to have it preserved within the family. But at whose expense? Father passed over ownership of the Hall to Berthold about twenty years ago, with a sum for its upkeep, but the sum declined in value while the upkeep grew in expense and, although Berthold has never complained on the matter, the building has been a burden on his resources for the better part of a decade. At the same time he has had his business problems which have become acute and his very large holding of shares in Hoch and Co. has become almost worthless. This does not, of course, mean that he has been rendered destitute but, given his commitments, he is no longer a rich man, and he hoped to realise something from the sale of the Hall. But now that a life-line has been thrown to him in the form of planning permission, you and your associates propose to cut it.

Berthold is not a wrecker. He is not going to pull down the Hall and leave a wilderness. He has plans for a housing estate. I have seen the sketches, which I take it, you have not. The houses blend in with their surroundings which the Hall, a great mass of Kensington baroque set down in an Essex meadow, does not. There is, moreover, a housing shortage in the area (which is why he finally got permission) and his plans would be fulfilling a social need which the Hall does not. On the other hand I will agree that the Hall is different, it is a landmark, it has got a history of sorts, and it may even be worth saving. What I cannot understand is your leading role in the movement to save it. You never expressed any affection for the place while it was still the family seat. On the contrary, you hated it and frequently complained, to use your inelegant expression, that it gave you 'the creeps' (whatever they might be). Celeste and I were always at a loss to explain what you had against it. It was spacious, it had lovely grounds, there were horses and dogs, everything a child loves. Father always made a fuss of you, and so, of course, did Gwendoline. Your mother thinks that you may have been troubled by the proportions of the place, and that it made you feel small and inadequate, but whatever the reasons we could never get you to share our affection of it. Why then should you of all people now be exerting yourself to save it?

You would not, I think, call me a severe or censorious parent. Your mother, indeed, has often complained that I was weak and indulgent, and she may have been right. Anyhow I feel I need no longer withhold from you the fact that in one way or another you have been a disappointment to us, but then I suppose I was a disappointment to my father, and disappointments tend to beget disappointments. Yet with all your ups and downs I have always consoled myself with the thought that you meant well and, as your aunt put it, 'it is sometimes better to mean well than to do well' (a precept, I may say, which has not always governed her own life), and certainly though I have known you to be imprudent, improvident and perhaps even thoughtless, I have never believed you could be malicious, but frankly, after reading about your Save-the-Hall campaign I am no longer so sure. It is certainly ironic that after so many years of inertia you should be applying your new-found energies to so harmful a cause. I take it you are also unaware what the family owes to your uncle.

Everybody knows how Father, the half-starved son of a Polish cobbler became a merchant prince, but hardly anybody knows that during the final decade of his life, he nearly destroyed everything he built up through suicidal stubbornness, and that Berthold had to run the business with one hand on the tiller and the other on Father. And my father was not the only burden he had to carry. There was yours also. I was called up to the army in the last months of the war and was gassed during a training exercise on Salisbury Plain. I have made a fairly complete recovery since (thanks to new drugs), but for the first ten years or so after the war I was in and out of hospital with various bronchial complaints and, whenever I was away Berthold was burdened with my work, always uncomplainingly and I also had the feeling that I was an even greater burden in the office than away from it.

He also looked after Gwendoline's affairs with rather greater care than his own, I would say, with the result that Gwendoline is now far better off than he'll ever be.

There is finally the effect your efforts are having on your mother's career. I don't know if you're aware of it, but your mother has taken on a new lease of life since we came here, and is in the throes of a campaign which has already made her a public figure, and she has only just started. There are people round here who feel she should stand for the Council if not for Parliament. Your efforts could have been almost expressly calculated to embarrass her. The fact that Berthold wants to demolish the Hall has already been seized on by the local papers, though the whole matter would have been forgotten had it not been fanned into life by your campaign.

May I ask you to call it off? I think you owe it to your uncle, your mother and perhaps even to me.

Your loving father,

Henry

Dear Mr Grosskopf,

I had the privilege of being at school with your late father and I believe you were the contemporary at the same school of my son Rodney. I don't know if you have kept in touch with him since, but I must tell you he has been less than a constant source of joy to us and I am particularly distressed by his present efforts to frustrate Berthold's plans to demolish Fetlock Hall, and sell the site for development. I wonder, therefore, if I could ask you to speak to Rodney for you may be able to bring home to him the gravity of the situation in a way that I could not. You might also hint that my fortunes are tied to those of Berthold and that if he cannot dispose of the site I may not be in a position to continue paying Rodney his monthly allowance. That, strictly speaking, may not be quite true, but what certainly is true is that if, as a result of Rodney's efforts, Berthold should not be able to proceed with his scheme, I most certainly shall cut off the allowance. I would hesitate to do so because it is my ultimate deterrent, and once used it becomes useless, but I cannot allow him to continue on his campaign of harassment unchallenged.

Yours sincerely

Henry Hoch

Chapter 6

Collapse of Stout Party

Dear Berthold,

I should imagine you have not heard of the Bor Shachor Progress and Development Party, which does not surprise me, for it only came into being in the early hours of yesterday morning under the chairmanship of your sister-in-law and my wife, Celeste Evelina Hoch.

We have so far functioned merely as the Bor Shachor Society and have approached each of the principal parties in the forthcoming municipal election, to see how far they were in sympathy with our aims. In general terms they were all for us, in particular terms they were all against us, and it became clear that if we hoped to get anywhere at all we would have to form our own party. So here we are.

All the parties in Bor Shachor belong to national groupings, are controlled by them and are bound to accept their policies no matter how they affect the local interest, and each local man accepts orders from on high because he is always anxious to rise with his party, and, of course, to rise in his party. People don't vote for individuals but for party lists, and we have decided to present our own list in the forthcoming elections. There are two dozen seats on the council and we are putting up two dozen candidates. We do not, of course, hope to have more than three or four returned, but that would be enough for our needs. The coalition is so shaky that any group with three or four votes at its disposal could be in a position to influence decisions and kill the tower blocks for good, or, at least, keep them out of our back garden. Celeste heads the list, then comes Nahumi, then comes Mic (or Michaeli) who is our campaign manager, then Gary. Humphry is eleventh or twelfth and the rest of the list is made up of his cousins. We have launched a half-a-million-pound fighting fund (which is about £50,000 sterling), which Humphry offered to organise, but we have asked him to keep out of it as we are a little afraid that he might rob a bank. Instead, we are writing to all our acquaintances and friends in various parts of the world who are rich or merely solvent, and who may sympathise with our aims. Gary is writing to friends in America, but if we should experience any difficulty in raising the money Celeste may fly out to Britain to form a committee of friends of Bor Shachor. We have over £10,000 in hand, most of it from our own lady bountiful, Gwendoline (bless her). We tried to persuade her to stand as one of our candidates. She doesn't speak a word of Hebrew, but she wouldn't have to, and her name on our list could in itself be worth a thousand votes, but she thought we were being frivolous.

The local parties are all well funded (there seems to be a shortage of money for everything here, except politics), and we can't hope to get started until we have substantial sums in the kitty (though Humphry has worked out that as there are only about twenty-five thousand voters on the local roll, it shouldn't cost more than £25,000 to buy the entire electorate, and probably less if we paid them in dollars). We are independent of all groups, a non-party party interested only in the welfare of Bor Shachor. We have no national ambitions and we are not directing our members how they should vote in the national elections. We are dividing the town into twenty-four wards, and undertake that each candidate will be the servant of his or her particular ward to deal with their complaints, look after their interests, help with their problems. In other words we're the people who care. Sounds glib, but we mean it.

But where, you may ask, do the tower blocks come in? In the small print, I'm afraid. Everybody's for them, so we can't say too loudly that we're against them, but we are saying that we shall preserve the Seraglio, and also that we intend to attract new investors and new investments, and as a start we shall unveil the plans for Gwendoline's hotel, the Fox and

Hounds. I have had a preview and strictly *entre nous*, they're appalling. Imagine a pocket-sized version of the Granada, Tooting, and you would have a building not unlike the Seraglio, which is a large Moorish-style villa of pink and yellow limestone. Into this she intends to introduce an olde worlde interior of oak beams and panels (probably of fibreglass) with alcoves and inglenooks, grained woodwork, stained ceilings, cast-iron fireplaces, and the end effect is something like a cross between the Cheshire Cheese and a neo-Georgian roadhouse. There is to be a long bar with all the usual impediments of pipes and taps. She intends to enrol Nicky as a barmaid (well, she does have the cleavage if nothing else). A pity poor Father isn't alive; she would have pulled him in as the oldest inhabitant. She will also have sporting prints round the walls (mainly, I gather, of the Aylesbury Hunt, which was patronised by the Rothschilds – thus introducing a Jewish element), and she is to import English beer by the barrel, so that it can be 'drawn from the wood', a mystique which is likely to be lost on the natives, or even, dare I say, on American tourists. It is all very vulgar and not at all in keeping with the character of Gwendoline (insofar as one knows her character) but a senior official of the Ministry of Tourism who saw her plans – she has already prepared a scale model – was hugging himself over them. 'It will be a goldmine without a doubt, a goldmine – people will come from the ends of the earth to stay here, especially Americans. English comforts and Israeli sunshine. Perfect.' The rooms, needless to say, are to have four-posters. If only one could have a ghost. Perhaps she'll supply that too.

Humphry, now that the weather is a little cooler, has begun sporting a waistcoat, which makes two of us thus attired in this country. His hair which, if you will remember, was convict's stubble, has now grown a little and he parts it in the middle. He has also grown a moustache, quite a bushy affair, which extends down the sides of his mouth like a thick trickle of gravy, and he is beginning to look like a Victorian waiter in his Sunday best. If Gwendoline could be induced to wear crinolines they would, I think, look just right together. Her taste in dress is still a little bizarre, especially her formal gowns which hang from her like expensive drapes and, what is worse, every little local dressmaker has been copying her styles, which she, at least, has the height to carry, but which the local matrons, who tend to be squat, have not, but they still entail a certain distinctiveness and I can foresee the evolution at what might be called the Bor Shachor look.

If we can save the Seraglio we can be certain of the hotel which, in spite of its compact size, would provide a considerable number of jobs, for Gwendoline will expect her clientele to be served hand and foot (she also plans to pick up guests arriving at Lud airport with a coach and horses), but, the hotel apart, we have to be careful with our promises, not only because we intend to keep them, but because we can only fall back on ourselves.

The others can use their party connections to get money for this or that project from the central government. We, of course, have no such connections. The money would have to be raised locally, and there is very little of it in this neighbourhood, and I suppose if we swept the board and actually won control we would be in a bit of a fix. Everybody tells me there's no chance of that, but with Celeste in charge I'm not so sure.

Yours ever,
Henry

Dear Berthold,

I always thought that Celeste was a fairly active being but Gwendoline has made her look comatose in comparison, and, as you say, marriage must have released new energies in her, or at least it has turned old energies – which she mainly applied to recrimination – to better use. A number of things troubled her about Bor Shachor, and the first of them was the cats. Well, the cats, lean, verminous, mangy, skulking, half-wild, half-starved brutes, looking more like shaggy ferrets than the pampered creatures we know at home, infest the place, but when an attempt was made to put them down about ten years ago they gave way to an even worse plague of rats. Anyway, Gwendoline came out with a two-stage plan, the first of which was to doctor the cats. When the mayor objected that he had no allocation in the budget for the purpose, she

hired her own vet and her own cat-catcher. The whole operation might take a fortnight, she thought. It took the better part
of three months. 'I hadn't imagined one small town could
support so many cats,' she said. It couldn't. What happened
was that the catcher (abetted by the vet), having exhausted the
local cat supply, began to bring in cats from as far afield as
Ashdod to the south and Jaffa to the north, before he was
caught out.

The second stage was to arrange a cat-show, to be held
three months hence, which will be open only to non-pedigree
animals (an unnecessary provision, for I doubt if there is a
pedigree cat south of Tel Aviv) with a free trip to Europe for
the owner of the supreme champion. As everybody here
dreams of a free trip to anywhere, there has been a run on
cats and there is hardly one to be seen in the streets.

Did I tell you that we have a local cricket team? It's my
own contribution to civilisation, though I will admit that it
only assumed active life after Humphry returned from England, where he had seen the game both on the village green at
Fetlock and at Lord's. Humphry took me to a football match
once – Bor Shachor v. Sodom, a second division match. The
referee was maimed by a missile and carried off in the opening minutes of the game, and what followed was a free-for-
all with kicks directed at everything except the ball. I am not
quite sure how many goal-keepers were on the pitch for everybody seemed to be handling the ball and there were moments
when the game looked like a particularly uncouth form of
rugby. 'What did you expect?' said Celeste when I told her
about it, 'Cricket?' And I thought to myself, why not? And
so I imported some cricket kit at great expense and at great
inconvenience, for when I went to collect it at Ashdod I had
the usual run around and more, for it was in the charge of
a custom's official who insisted that it constituted neither
educational supplies nor sports goods, but furnishings, and that
I must pay duty on it as such. 'It's a game,' I almost screamed,
and showed him the balls which he then removed from their
package and threw them on the ground. 'Balls, are they, eh?'
he demanded triumphantly. 'If they're balls, why not they
bounce?'

One of course needs more than cricket kit for cricket, and I had to pull both Celeste and Nahumi into the game before I could get as much as a team together, let alone an opposing side. We didn't in fact take off till Humphry returned from England and enrolled an entire generation of younger cousins as trainees. They tended, at first, to handle their bats as if they were playing baseball, but they learned quickly, even to exclaiming 'howzat'! every time a ball was bowled. ('Howzat!' has, indeed, become something like a local refrain and is employed in situations very far removed from cricket.)

Last week we had a match against Givat Schmertz, a local kibbutz with a considerable number of South African and English chaps. It was not without its difficult moments. First of all, Humphry, who captained our team (and who emerged beautifully arrayed like a beardless W. G. Grace) fielded something like twenty-five players, and when the opposing side complained he insisted that the surplus figures were merely spectators who wanted a close view of the game. Next, the wicket-keeper had to be sent off after he contrived to get the batsman out before the ball had even been bowled. Then there was the strange episode in which two (or even three) balls appeared to be in play at the same time, one of which Humphry claimed to have caught and which the batsman claimed not to have hit. The umpire, an English bank clerk from Tel Aviv, was confounded by the whole incident, but having ruled against the home team in the wicket-keeping episode, ruled for it on this occasion and Givat Schmertz walked off the field. It was, I think, Matthew who induced them to come back and they went on to score about six hundred runs. The real trouble came during our innings. Humphry went in first and was out with the very first ball. He insisted, however, that the proper signal to play had never been given and that he was still adjusting his pads when he looked up to see the stumps flying in all directions.

'I'm sorry,' said the umpire, 'you're out.'

'Out?' said Humphry.

'Out,' said the umpire.

'I want a second opinion,' said Humphry. 'This umpire is on their side, I want an umpire on our side.' And we decided to adjourn for tea while the matter was settled. In the end a com-

promise was reached. Humphry was prevailed upon to withdraw his demands for another umpire, while Givat Schmertz,
who I must say were an extremely patient and sporting lot,
agreed to overlook their first ball, but when we returned to
the pitch somebody had stolen the stumps, as well as one of the
bats and we had to have another adjournment while I brought
replacements.

The crowd which had been thin at the beginning of the
game now grew to considerable proportions and Humphry got
a loud and sustained cheer as he went in to resume his innings,
but, alas, came the first ball and he was out lbw.

'What the hell do you mean, lbw?' said Humphry, advanc-
ing menacingly on the umpire, 'It hit me between the legs.'

'Yes, but the principle's the same.'

'Is it? I don't know what you have between your legs, but
what I have isn't a leg.'

'That's immaterial.'

'Not what I have isn't.'

'Whatever it may be was in front of the wicket.'

'It makes no difference whether it was before the wicket
or after the wicket, or under the wicket. It wasn't a leg. You
want to see?'

'No, that shouldn't be necessary.'

'Good, so no more interruptions, please.'

'The fact remains – '

The crowd couldn't quite take in what was happening. As
far as they could see their hero was being penalised for nothing,
and as the argument continued they invaded the pitch. I am
not quite sure what happened next, but within minutes several
jeeploads of policemen came roaring onto the scene and began
swinging clubs in all directions, and it was only when a sergeant
found himself crowning the sacrosanct head of a kibbutznick
that he called his men off and cleared the pitch. By then
another set of stumps had disappeared, as had the bats and
ball, and the game was finally abandoned.

It was, with all the commotion and mayhem, a welcome
distraction from politics.

Yours ever,
Henry

Dear Berthold,

The two Chief Rabbis of Bor Shachor descended on us this morning in one joint delegation – the first time I have seen them act in unison – the one bowler-hatted, the other in a homburg. And both with the same complaint. We were undermining Judaism in Bor Shachor. How? Why? Your Party, they replied with one voice. But we had hardly launched it. News travels fast, said Rabbi one. Especially bad news, said Rabbi t'other. You are inviting a calamity, they said together.

Rabbi Mittwoch took over as spokesman.

'My learned friend and I are holy vessels – not to mix in politics, but when you kill the Holy Alliance you kill Judaism. You will have naked men and women in the swimming pool, your sons will marry idol worshippers, and you'll have buses in the street on the Holy Shabbat. Bor Shachor will become Sodom and Gomorrah. Because for why? Because you split the religious vote. And why the religious vote? Because you're known. You come to synagogue regular. You give money for charity. You are Anglo-Saxon respectable, and religious people respect respectable people. They vote for you, but not so many vote for you as to give you seats. No, what happens is the Holy Alliance lose seats, you win nothing, and the non-religious win everything, so they have a swimming pool with naked people, and buses in the street on the Holy Shabbat. You make a big mistake and bring a calamity on the whole House of Israel, God forbid.'

'Amen,' said his colleague, who lingered behind after the other had left to ask what I had against him. Nothing, I said. Then why, he demanded almost tearfully, did I bring his colleague a magnificent bowler hat from London and not him? Hasn't he got a head? A fair question. Isn't he a chief Rabbi? Will you be in St James' in the near future? If so, could you pop into Lock's and pick up a bowler? His size is $7\frac{1}{2}$ but as the bowler is worn about the ears round here you'd better make it $7\frac{3}{4}$.

Hardly had the holy men left when we were visited by no less a person than His Worship the Mayor (recently back from a study mission), a large, hearty man with what we used to call a substantial 'corporation', except that in England corporations are – or at least were – contained behind a well-tailored waistcoat. His worship, however, being an ex-kibbutznick, goes about in a short-sleeved, open-necked shirt, and his corporation almost threatens to spill over.

'I come to congratulate you for your manifesto. I know it isn't published yet, but publication in Bor Shachor is an extravagance. Everybody here knows everything before it happens. If I was a voter living in Bor Shachor I would vote for you.'

'But you are a voter living in Bor Shachor,' Celeste pointed out.

'True, true, but we are saying almost the same, only we said it first. We want everything you want – '

'We don't want tower blocks,' said Celeste.

'Do you think I do? They darken the eye. They're a plague and a pestilence. They're not economic, not in a place like this where land is cheap and labour isn't. They're Donegal's dream, but he's an astute politician. The people want them and, if word got around that the Holy Alliance wanted the towers and we didn't, Donegal would be the next mayor. No, everybody wants towers now, right, left, centre, but not everybody wants a swimming pool. What happens in the very hot weather? People with cars, like you or me or Donegal, drive down to the beach, or belong to a swimming club, or have friends in a kibbutz – and of course nearly every kibbutz has a swimming pool. But what do the people, the working men, without cars or friends in the kibbutz, what do they do? They sit and swelter in their slums. We work a six-day week here. Their only free day is the Shabbat, when they can't even take a bus to the beach, because as you know the buses don't run on the Shabbat.'

'I am not sure that I would want buses to run on Shabbat.'

'But cars – '

'If I had my way I'd stop them too. I have every sympathy with these zealots who heave bricks at passing traffic on the Sabbath. I often feel tempted to do the same on weekdays.'

'But you drive – '

'We have a car, we use it rarely, but I would willingly forgo the use of it, if others would forgo theirs. There is no more lethal creature than an Israeli behind the wheel. I have never travelled up to Jerusalem or Tel Aviv without seeing mangled cars and blood on the roadways. I know cars are popular and those that don't have them regard themselves as prospective motorists in temporarily deprived circumstances. I'm sure if I offered every voter a raffle ticket in a Mercedes we'd sweep the board, but I am not a believer in giving the public what they want – '

'Do you think I am? But I give them some of the things that they want in order that they should accept other things which I think they should have. My name is Rafi, but you know what people round here call me?'

'Abba.'

'Exactly. Father. They trust me. I built this place. It isn't quite Athens, or as my friend Donegal would say, even Limerick, but you don't know what it was before I came here, or what it could be if I didn't have the Holy Alliance breathing down my collar – '

'We've just been told that we'd undermine the Holy Alliance,' I said.

'Nothing can undermine them, unfortunately. They always get the same vote from the same people. The Rabbis tell them how to vote and they vote. And as the Rabbis are appointed by the Holy Alliance they vote for the Holy Alliance. It's become a custom with them, like wearing a hat. No, no. If you take away votes they'll be ours. We are the people who want progress in Bor Shachor, and have brought progress to it, and I'll tell you why. Who lives here? People who couldn't get to anywhere else. Moroccans who couldn't get into France, Libyans who couldn't get into Italy, Romanians who couldn't make it to America. Sure, there's a few idealists, who came to this country at great sacrifice, people like me, Donegal maybe, a few others and you, of course. Not because you're from the West. Not every Ango-Saxon who comes here is a flaming idealist. We get all sorts, struck-off doctors, unfrocked lawyers, bankrupt businessmen, people on the run, husbands absconding from their wives, wives from their husbands, children from their parents, parents from their children, crazy Americans looking for the Messiah, crazier Americans who think they are the Messiah. You're not on the run. You're not bankrupt. You've got money, you're from a good family. You have roots in England. In fact, when you first settled here you caused a great deal of puzzlement. People began to wonder why, what you were up to, and as somebody said to me : "If they're sane, they must be crazy." You're admired. You have a nice house, a nice car, you dress nicely. Your sister in particular is looked upon as a princess, and Humphry is a folk hero, the local boy who's made good. They fill the papers. People will vote for you, not many, but enough for us to lose two or three seats, and, if we lose, Donegal becomes mayor, and if Donegal becomes Mayor Bor Shachor goes back to the Middle Ages. Don't misunderstand me, I like Donegal. He is a nice little man personally, but politically he's a disaster, because he and his party are always looking over their shoulder at the Ultra Orthodox, because no matter how religious you are in this country, there's always someone to your right who thinks you're a *goy*. For the moment they're content with stopping the buses on Shabbat and keeping the swimming pool dry, but if they get into power they'll stop all life. If you'll excuse me, you'll not be able to pass water on the Shabbat. As it is, you don't know the trouble I have keeping the public lavatories open. I told the Rabbis plainly, if bowels will close on Shabbat then I'll close the lavatories. Then there's the weekly battle over the cafés. You've got families of ten or twelve living in two or three rooms in this town, so what do they do at night? They take to the streets, the cafés, the pictures, a discotheque. On Friday almost everything is closed except a café or two, and they want me to close them. I haven't the power, I tell them. Use the fire regulations, they say. Fire regulations! If I enforced the fire regulations the first buildings I'd have to close are the synagogues.

'Would you allow freedom of worship?' Celeste asked. He looked at her blankly.

'Where in Israel isn't there freedom of worship?'

'There isn't in Bor Shachor for a start, not if you're a Reform Jew – '

'Ah, you mean Gittleson.'

'I do, and don't bring up the excuse of it being a place of

special architectural and historical importance, I'll take that from Donegal, but not from you.'

'Give me a chance, I haven't said anything. Sure, I know all about that, and it's a scandal, but it's part of the price I have to pay for having Donegal as a partner.'

'If you won control would you allow Gary to proceed?'

'Certainly, except that of course Israel is a small country, and things you do in one place have repercussions in another, and if I was seen to give open encouragement to a Reform congregation in Bor Shachor, I could embarrass the party at large. Don't forget more than half of the Jews here – and about seventy per cent of the population of Bor Shachor – come from North Africa and Asia. They've never had a Reform movement there and have no idea what it's about. To them you're either an Orthodox Jew who keeps everything, or a sinner who doesn't. They can't understand the Jew who tries to adapt the creed to his beliefs, and what they don't understand they don't like. I have to keep all that in mind.'

'Which is all the more reason why we should fight the election as a non-party group.'

'My dear, there is no such thing as a non-party group. A party is a group who come together to get things done, and if they find they're getting nowhere they join another group, which gets them somewhere. That's why I'm in the Workers' League, to get things done. Your group will do nothing for itself, it will only harm us. You'll find that out for yourself, and when you do then you'll join us, and I'll forgive you, I'll even welcome you with open arms, but why not join us now before you've done harm?'

'What do you mean?'

'I want you to merge your group with ours, that's what I mean. I'm going to make you an offer you can't refuse.'

There were twenty-four seats on the council, of which the League never won less than eight and sometimes as many as eleven. He offered to make Celeste number seven on his list which would virtually assure her a seat. 'It will bring you to the heart of power,' he told her. 'You're a very persuasive woman, but you're using your power in the wrong way and the wrong place. Even if you win two or three seats as a group, which you won't – '

'Who says we won't?'

'I say you won't.'

'I'm not so sure.'

'Right. Have it your way. Supposing you do win four seats, it will be almost entirely at our expense, which will make Donegal's the largest party, but not large enough to rule, so it'll be another coalition, and if there is, you will either be part of the ruling clique – and I can see him offering you a job as Deputy Mayor – in which case you can forget about the Seraglio and the pool and everything else you stand for, or you'll be out of it, in which case you'll be powerless to do anything in the first place, but if you had a place in the League – '

'Is the *you* singular or plural?'

'What do you mean?'

'I'm not the only member of my party.'

'We would look after your colleagues.'

'And the towers?'

'About them we can talk.'

'Well, talk.'

'Not now.'

'When?'

'After the elections. For the time being it's settled. The people want them, and the people shall have them. They're the bread and circuses.'

'On the present site.'

'That's a detail, there we can talk.'

'I thought it was a *fait accompli.*'

'Some *faits* are more *accomplis* than others. Look, once they begin work on the site somebody might find water, or oil, or a royal tomb. You never know what you can turn up in this country once you dig a hole in the ground.'

'I thought it was surveyed.'

'So we'll re-survey it. You can't start rushing up twenty-two storey tower blocks just anywhere. There may be some complications because the company has been given the go-ahead, but we can tell them that we're planning some new immigrant housing scheme nearby, or even factories and they may prefer another site. There's always room for manoeuvre. We can talk about it.' He put a hand on Celeste's knee.

'Well, what do you think?'

'I think I should like to think about it.'

What would you do, Berthold?

Yours ever,
Henry

Dear Berthold,

I don't know what dear Gwendoline's been writing to you. It's true that she has had some *contretemps* with Celeste, but the fault has been entirely hers. The fact that she is now a married woman has not made her any the less wilful or naïve.

It is completely untrue that we have 'betrayed her and the cause'. She was a latecomer to the cause in the first place. Celeste was campaigning to save the Seraglio and against the towers long before Gwendoline had heard of either. Second of all, Celeste is still determined to save the one, and fend off the other, but has merely changed tactics. The local political parties have been in business for a long time. All have their ears to the ground, and if they have one thing in common, it's their attitude to the towers. They're for them. If we were to come out against them we would be finished before we started, and we have therefore left them out of our programme. This is not opportunism, but realism. If Celeste was an opportunist, she could have got a high place on the ruling party list which would have assured her a place on the council, and, what is more important, a say in the policies of the ruling party.

Nor is it true to say that we have come out in favour of tower blocks. It's merely that she refuses to be dogmatic. She was against the demolition of the Seraglio and the erection of a tower on its site, and she's still against it, but she has never suggested that towers *per se* are a crime against humanity, and if the public wants them, need one be so elitist as to turn round and tell them, no, you can't have them, they're not good for you, as if ratepayers were small children demanding sweets?

Tower blocks also have a psychological effect, they raise aspirations, widen horizons, give new perspectives. One wouldn't want Bor Shachor to become another New York but, as Celeste says, a lofty block here and there, well spaced, can give dignity to a place. The trouble with Celeste is that she's always willing to see reason, the trouble with Gwendoline is that she's not. We take her displeasure to be temporary. She threatened us with the cancellation of the hotel plan, and C, never one to be threatened, said: 'Do, by all means,' which was a little rash, for in fact the hotel plan is central to our whole scheme. Celeste said that if Gwendoline withdrew she'd find somebody else to take it over, and half threatened to do it herself, though, of course, we haven't got that sort of money. And if we fail to get even a nominal foothold on the council the Seraglio is lost, and the hotel plan with it. It is, of course, difficult to talk to her when she's in one of her moods, but you can sometimes make her see sense, and I wonder, therefore, if I could ask you to write to her, or better still, phone her.

> Yours ever,
> Henry

Dear Berthold,

Celeste took your advice and wrote to Gerald about the hotel. She did so reluctantly for she was saving him for another pet project, of which more later, but she told him the whole story, the difficulties with Gwendoline, how the plan was complete and that all that was needed was a miserly million dollars to see the thing through. It was, she assured him – and dispatched a mass of figures to prove it – a solid investment with solid prospects.

He replied in a long cable that one of his subsidiaries had already sunk a million dollars in some development deal in Israel and that the whole thing was loused up because some crazy old dame had thrown herself across the roadway and wouldn't let the trucks pass. In America, he said, the trucks would have gone over her, or, if not, she would have been bundled into an ambulance and put away for life. The word 'action', he complained, meant nothing in Israel, promises meant nothing and he wouldn't invest another cent. I'd rather give away a million dollars and forget about it than invest a thousand and have recurring headaches. 'Not another (if you will excuse the language) fucking cent.'

And what was this development deal? None other than the Bor Shachor towers. But, as I reminded her, wasn't there a time when Gerald was looking into the possibility of buying the Seraglio for his own use? There was, she said, but obviously he didn't know that one of his own subsidiaries had already bought it. I knew he had a large empire but it hadn't occurred to me – or perhaps to him – that it was that large. So there we have it, our own dear brother at the source of our whole trouble, and my own dear wife at the source of his.

Celeste has flown to New York.

Yours,
Henry

Dearest Celeste,

I don't know what headway you are making with Gerald, but I can report a triumph at home, due mainly to the efforts of Humphry (may his tribe increase!). He has fallen in love with the idea of being Mine Host at the Fox and Hounds, to say nothing of his place on a party list, even if it carries little hope of a seat on the council. He had only to sulk for a week before Gwendoline gave in, though the fact that you didn't happen to be around also helped. If I may so, dear, you're not a woman's woman, at least not where Gwendoline is concerned, and you do tend to rub her up the wrong way (though to be sure one can never be certain of how to rub her up the right way). Anyway, if all is not quite smiles, all is understanding and the hotel is back in our plan. If you should at the same time persuade Gerald to drop the tower scheme we'll have won without a shot being fired and we could relax a bit, which would be rather nice, don't you think? We didn't bargain for the rush and bustle when we made our home here and it would be pleasant to get back to a calmer, less hectic atmosphere. Nahumi and I have been celebrating the happy turn of events in Kapulski's with innumerable cups of coffee and complete slabs of *Apfelstrudel.*

My dear, I have made Rodney see reason which, I think you will agree, is no small accomplishment. He has withdrawn from the campaign to save the Hall (though the campaign itself, alas, appears to be continuing).

All my love,
Henry

Dear Berthold,

I love my wife, but I'm not sure I understand her. She returned from America in triumph bearing everything she wanted, and a bit more besides. Gerald agreed to withdraw his investments from the Seraglio site and transfer it elsewhere. Which is to say, Bor Shachor is to have its towers, but not where they poke the eye.

He is also, believe it or not, to pay for a Bor Shachor opera. Celeste had intended to appeal to his filial piety by calling it the Solomon Hoch Memorial Opera House, but decided to appeal to his vanity instead and it is to be known as the Gerald M. Higham Opera Centre. I can't think of anything more ridiculous, but Nahumi said, 'Ziss will put Bor Shachor on ze maps,' and when I pointed out that no one in Bor Shachor could tell Wagner from the Wizard of Oz, he said, 'Ah yes, but people become educated, yes? Zey come from Tel Aviv and Ashdod to listen. We make it with restaurant, good music, good food, good wine, zey go together.'

'But you need good taste to start with,' I said.

'We teach zem.'

The whole idea is, of course, still in embryo form but Celeste envisages it as a sort of Glyndebourne, set amid orchards and trees among which people could picnic between acts.

I frankly think that a Bor Shachor opera is about as practical an idea as a Bor Shachor hunt (if anything, the latter is possibly the more practical for Gwendoline has in fact been talking about it, and wouldn't Humphry make a superb Jorrocks?). Still, let me not diminish my dear wife's achievements. It is something to get Gerald to part with a million dollars on any pretext and had I been the Queen I would have given her the Garter.

We had a small party and Nahumi made a toast to the triumph of the Bor Shachor Progress and Development Party, which now seems assured. He continued at some length holding his glass aloft in a palsied hand till its contents were all over him. 'In times to come,' he concluded, 'people will look back on our dear Celeste as zey do now on the prophetesses Deborah and Huldah, but to us she is more than a prophetess, she is our Queen. I give you ze toast to ze queen of Bor Shachor.'

At which point the Queen rose to confound us all. *She wants to dissolve the party!* I thought I hadn't heard her right, neither had anyone else. 'We've got everything we want,' she explained. 'We must get out of that awful Jewish habit of keeping something going even after it has outlived its use. I believe in political euthanasia.'

'But zis is not euthanasia, zis is murder,' said Nahumi. 'We have everything we want because we are organised, if we become disorganised everything is lost.'

'And we haven't everything we want,' said Gary, 'there's the pool, there's the Reform synagogue.'

'I haven't forgotten them,' said Celeste, 'but we have a better chance of getting them by working as a pressure group.'

'No, no, no.' Poor Nahumi danced round the floor with vexation. 'We have gone over zis again and again, and we agree to form ze party because here everysing is parties.'

'But we have to be practical,' said Celeste. 'If we stand as an independent group we may get two or three seats, all at the expense of the League – '

'Why do you say zat?'

'You worked it out yourself.'

'Maybe two seats at ze ezpense of ze League.'

'Even with two, the League could be reduced to seven, even six, which could let Donegal in as senior partner, but even if he remains junior partner you could forget about the synagogue and the pool.'

'But how would staying out help?' asked Gary.

'Well,' said Celeste, lighting a cigarette, 'I wasn't suggesting that we stay out altogether. My idea is that we should become a pressure group within the League.'

'How?' said several voices.

'By a merger.'

Collapse of stout party.

Yours ever,
Henry

Chapter 7

The Candidate

Dear Berthold,

What you read in the *Jewish Chronicle* about Celeste is only too true, and no doubt you will soon be reading it in *The Times* for Abba has stood down in her favour and she is to head the Workers' League and, unless something goes very wrong with the fortunes of the League, she will be the next mayor of Bor Shachor and the first woman mayor in Israel. Hence all the publicity.

This is how it happened. Celeste commissioned a local poll which showed that we would get four, or possibly even five, seats in the next election, that the League representation would be reduced to seven or even six, which would have put Donegal in as mayor. In fact it confirmed all the worst fears of Abba, but at the same time it gave her a powerful bargaining position, and Abba offered her the second place on the list.

'I think,' she said, 'that you can do better than that.'

'You don't want to be mayor of this wretched place, do you?' he asked, in what he thought was a rhetorical question.

'I don't,' she said, 'on the other hand, we would be making political history, and can you imagine the attention it would bring to Bor Shachor – the first town in Israel to have a woman mayor? My topping the list could be worth five thousand votes to us.'

'My name also stands for something in this town, you know,' said Abba.

'A great deal, but you've been mayor now for twenty years. The public is fickle and all the indications are that they want a change, and if our party doesn't offer it they could turn to Donegal.'

'Who in his senses would vote for him?'

'No one, but there are many people with votes and without sense. This way you could step down with dignity while you're still at the top, of your own accord. In the other you might be toppled and it would be a sad end to a lifetime of service.' Upon which Abba threw up his hands and gave way.

The news spread like wildfire and Abba hardly left before Donegal was on the doorstep.

'Tell me it isn't true,' he pleaded half-tearfully. 'You haven't, you haven't thrown in your lot with the *goyim*? If you have, all I've done for Bor Shachor is finished. There'll be no Shabbos, no Yom Tov. The Yeshiva will shrink and pull out. No God-fearing Jew will want to live here. It will become a place of low resort. You'll have discotheques blaring from every corner, day and night, Shabbat and Yom Tov. You'll have sex shops in the high street and pornography in the school playgrounds. If the Holy Alliance is out everything is open to lewdness and corruption. You'll have pork in your Wimpeys, and horse-meat in your sausages! You'll not know what's kosher and what isn't, for you'll have no one to supervise the supervisors. And that's only the beginning. Give a place a bad name and it's in business. You'll have low-class cabarets and night clubs opening up in every back street, and places whose character I wouldn't describe in the presence of a lady. Jaysus Christ if it's position you're after, why didn't you come to me in the first place?'

'Because it's not position I'm after,' said Celeste.

'Then what the hell are you after? You didn't want the towers in your back garden, you won't have them –'

'The pool –'

'We could have talked about that.'

'The Reform synagogue.'

'Yes, even the bloody Reform synagogue. We could have talked about it.'

'We did talk about it, if you recall, and you said it couldn't be done.'

'Sure it couldn't be done, but you weren't holding a pistol

to my head then. It never occurred to me that you'd be going over to the other side.'

'I haven't gone over to them,' said Celeste. 'They've come over to us.'

About an hour later the two Rabbis arrived ashen-faced, each bearing a brown paper parcel. They were returning their bowlers.

'I want you to know', said Rabbi Mittwoch in a husky voice, 'it is against the law for a woman to be a Queen in Israel, for it is written in the Holy Torah, "Thou shalt set a King over thee", and'when it says that thou shalt set a King it means thou shalt not set a Queen. A Queen is forbidden.'

'It also says', retorted Celeste drily, 'that thou shalt honour thy father and thy mother; does that mean that thou mayest not honour thy maiden aunt?'

'A mayor isn't quite the same as a Queen,' I added.

'The same, the same,' said Mittwoch. 'It is wrong, it is forbidden. It is a misfortune. Yours sons will marry idol worshippers, you will have buses in the swimming pools and naked people in the streets on the Holy Shabbat.'

In short he was rather upset. I'm not sure that I wasn't, for I dislike upsetting people – even Rabbis – and we are in danger of losing all our friends, if, indeed, we have not already lost them. Dear old Nahumi will have nothing more to do with her, and it doesn't look as if he wants to have all that much to do with me.

Gary too is upset. She had taken him aside to point out that it wouldn't help to introduce the matter of Reform in the election. 'They just can't associate Reform with synagogues,' she explained, 'it's a contradiction in terms, and it would just muddle the electorate and get Donegal votes. Why don't you just go ahead and convert your house without asking any questions? Everybody does it.'

'But isn't it against the law?'

'I'm not sure that it is, but the best way of finding out is to do it. In any case they've never taken action over our conversion, so you have at least one precedent to work on.'

'Yes, but you see it's a synagogue I'm trying to build, and if I should start on the wrong foundations I'm not sure if we can expect anything else to go right.'

'That's all we need in Bor Shachor,' she said to me later, 'a saint.'

Humphry has come along with us, and is number nine on the list, which gives him reasonable hope of a seat, and while Gwendoline is not too happy about his involvement (for she does not trust Celeste) she is a good loyal wife and graces the platform at most of our major meetings, and I must say she is an attraction – a little like having the Queen Mother on one's side. Celeste, I'm afraid, is not looking her best and has become less than her immaculate self. She has given up her weekly visit to the hairdresser. She has abandoned her Queen Mary style with her hair piled neatly on top. Instead she has let it grow and more often than not gathers it up in a bun at the back. She smokes heavily. Her fingers have become stained and she is covered in ash. Her eyes sag. People talk of her as if she was another Margaret Thatcher, but in fact she looks more like Harold Macmillan. She has, however, become an accomplished speaker and harangues her audiences in Hebrew, French, English and even bits of Yiddish – where did she pick *that* up? She raises her voice, flails her arms, weaves her thumb, stabs the air with her forefinger and sometimes gets so worked up that one half expects her to take off. And the campaign has not even opened (at least officially, though there is in fact no closed season for electioneering round here).

What, I keep asking myself, has brought her to this? I can't recall that she even as much as voted at elections in England. She grumbled at things, but then so did I and there can hardly be an issue on which I have not out-grumbled her. Is there something about the air of Israel which does it to one? Well, whatever it is, it hasn't done it to me, yet. She has, of course, always had a natural authority about her, and it may just be that Israel gave her an opportunity to exercise it which England did not, but I often watch her perform and keep wondering whether she could be the woman I married over forty years ago and whose previous public commitments rarely extended beyond the Isleworth branch of the League of Jewish Women.

Yours ever,
Henry

Dear Berthold,

Disaster! There was a short piece about Celeste in the *New York Times* which came to Gerald's attention. I don't know how, for as far as I'm aware he reads nothing but cables and balance sheets. Anyhow it gave him the impression that Celeste was a raging Bolshevik. I suppose it was the name 'the Workers' League' which did it, anyway there arrived on Celeste's desk a cable bearing the words: RESENT YOUR LINK WITH REDS STOP WITHDRAWING FROM OPERA. Celeste replied as best as the exigencies of cableese would permit, without getting a reply. Finally she managed to get hold of Gerald on the phone, and then discovered that it was not only the *NY Times* report which troubled him, but something he had been told by our friend, Donegal.

'Look,' he said, 'I'm no saint. I'm hardly ever in synagogue, but when I do go I like to find it as it always was, without any innovations, or any of that Liberal Reform crap. Jesus Christ, if you can't depend on your fucking religion to stay fixed, what's left? Change at every fucking turn. Well, I don't want any changes in the fucking synagogues. I want them to be the real thing, Orthodox. If you want Reform shit there's plenty of it in America, you don't have to go to Israel for that. Do you know what I always do when I'm in London, do you?'

Celeste hesitated to offer a suggestion.

'I go to synagogue. Surprises you, doesn't it? – 'cause I hardly ever go in New York, but I go to the New West End where Dad used to take us when we were boys, and it's there as it always was, the same interior, the same tunes, the same traditions, even the same smells – I'd have burned the fucking place down if it had been any different. The Rabbi looked the same, he dressed the same, he sounded the same. And that's another thing. What have you been doing to the poor, fucking Rabbis?'

'Me?'

'Yes, you and the other reds, you've been breaking their fucking hearts. Don't holy men mean nothing to you? Is nothing fucking sacred? Who keeps the old store going if not them? What'll happen to my grandchildren and yours when they'll want to savour authentic Judaism, and I mean the real thing, not the *ersatz* shit served up in the Reform temples. There'll be nothing left if you give a free run to those Reform creeps. Half of them are Commies in the first place, marching to Georgia for the schwartzes, marching on Washington against Vietnam, while their fucking million dollar temples stayed empty. It's kosher-style Christianity, is that what you want to start in Israel? Jesus Christ, if Father was alive he would have risen from his grave.'

'Look Gerald, I am not a theologian, but one of the things I do believe in is justice.'

'Christ, do you think I don't? That's why I'm against all that Reform crap, it's an injustice to authentic Judaism. You've got to suffer it here in America because it's always been here, but why do you want to start with it in Israel?'

'I don't want to start anything.'

'You're building a Reform temple.'

'I'm not.'

'I've got it here in front of me, it's all in the fucking paper.'

'Never believe what you read in the papers.'

'Yes, but even if half of it is true – '

'Half of a lie isn't a truth. I am not trying to build Reform temples but there are Reform Jews who are as sincere about their beliefs as you are about yours.'

'Beliefs? I've got no beliefs, I've got sentiments, and I've got respect for antiquity. These creeps want to change every-thing – '

'They want to change nothing, all they want is a place where they can meet for prayer – '

'Let them meet in church.'

Celeste saw no point in further argument and put down the receiver with a look of despair on her face.

Is an opera house all that important?' I asked.

'It is to me. I don't intend to build a political career on broken promises.'

Abba suggested that she could go on a fund-raising tour of America after the elections. As Israel's first woman mayor every door and every pocket would be opened to her.

'No,' she said, 'it's in our programme. I've promised it.

We've got a lot of publicity for it and not a few sniggers. It's the sniggers which still ring in my ear. I mean to find the money.'

'What? Now?'

'Now.'

Abba looked at me as if to say, 'Does she always act like this?' And then he exploded.

'You're mad. The campaign opens in another week and you're going to chase around the globe raising a million dollars for an opera! Bor Shachor needs an opera like I need a hole in the head.'

'You'll probably get one if you go on like this. You were all for it, why the sudden change?'

'I was all for the million dollars. A million dollars means jobs, and if the opera was the only way to get it, I was all for it. If someone offered a million for a cat and dog home I'd be for it too.'

'A promise is a promise.'

'Now look, you're not on the hustings now. You're talking to an old pro. You got into this whole game because you were against tower blocks, but you've dropped that. You were for a Reform synagogue, you've dropped that – you've dropped almost everything in your original programme, so why hold on to the opera?'

'Because', I suggested, 'she has to hold on to something.'

'Will you keep out of this Henry, please?'

'Why, tell me, why?'

'Because I have been particularly identified with the opera.'

'But nobody takes it seriously. Everybody thinks it's a gimmick to catch the headlines, everybody, the papers, our opponents, even our friends.'

'Which is precisely why I mean to find the money.'

And you know, Berthold, as she said that, I felt a slight chill go through me. There is something a little frightening about such determination.

Yours ever,
Henry

Dear Berthold,

You will have received Celeste's unfortunate letter by now, and no doubt you have drawn the same sad conclusions as I have. Ambition has gone to her head! She wants to put the entire family trust in hock to raise £400,000 from the banks. She is confident that either Gerald will come to his senses or, if not, she will go on a fund-raising tour after the elections and find the money herself and that she will repay the sum in six months. I am rather less sanguine, and so, I take it, are you. I have, of course, withheld my signature. Surprisingly, however, Gwendoline has given hers (I have given up trying to discover how her mind works – perhaps it simply doesn't), and if you could add yours then she can do what she likes and will probably ruin us all. That may, indeed, be her plan for she has become totally unscrupulous and when we are out in the streets, with our possessions sold, she may then turn to Gerald with a new appeal, not for the opera, but for his own dear family. Little does she know our Gerald. You know, one of the drawbacks of prosperity is a nagging sense of insecurity, the feeling that it can't, and perhaps it shouldn't, last – and I have been looking out for all sorts of disasters, wars, famines, revolutions. Little did I think that my own dear wife might be the source of our ruin. I don't know how you feel about your children. I love my children, and I think they love me, but I have no doubt whatever that if Celeste and I should find ourselves destitute they will not hesitate to put us in an old age home. I remember having this very thought twenty years ago when we endowed a ward in the Jewish Old Age Home in Mother's memory, and I said to you then, as we inspected the ancients on parade, that we may yet be the beneficiaries of our own generosity. And I thought I was joking.

Well, dear Berthold, with Celeste as a wife many of the things one used to laugh at have ceased to be funny. I am distressed not only by the direction of her thought but by her manner. Our whole life has changed. She was never the most relaxed of individuals but we used to have a pleasant routine, going shopping together (did you know that she has induced our friendly neighbourhood nose-picking grocer to alter his premises and his habits and all is now washed hands and white tiles, and, alas, higher prices), popping into Stein-matzky's for the English papers, and then stopping to read them at Kapulski's with coffee cooling by our side. That has all stopped, so has the Bor Shachor cinema club, so have our outings to the Romanian restaurant. I do the shopping on my own, and she upbraids me for the ridiculous prices I pay, but then I have never learned to haggle, and I'm rather glad I haven't. More often that not I do the cooking, which doesn't trouble me, for I like dabbling in the kitchen, but it troubles her because I get my recipes from the back numbers of the English colour supplements which, as you know, are rather heavy on Cointreau. We used to sit out on the verandah as night began to fall and gaze out upon the distant hills changing colour in the setting sun, or to take in the night air. We hardly spoke, but sat there in a sublime and contented stupor, coming to life occasionally to smack a mosquito. That's all over. The house has become a committee room, with sweaty, shouting, gesticulating, shirt-sleeved figures, darting in all directions through a heavy haze of tobacco smoke. There are two toilets in the house and I can rarely get into either, so that I am often pressed to dash out into the garden and water the plants – and even there I keep being surprised by a skinny harridan in thick glasses who, I suspect, lies in wait for me. I hardly see anything of Celeste – and I don't always recognise her when I do. She is always in conference or addressing meetings. She is never in bed by the time I'm asleep and is up and about by the time I wake and I'm not even sure that she sleeps at all, and if it wasn't for the fact that the Sabbath still means something to her and that we still eat together on Friday nights, I don't think I would see anything of her from one end of the week to the other. I am in a way proud of her, but could do without her fame and achievements and am sorry that she got mixed up in the whole show. Indeed, I'm beginning to be sorry that we came out here in the first place. Happily, old Nahumi hasn't moved yet and we sit outside Kapulski's when we can find a place, he leaning on his stick and I on mine, shaking our heads, commiserating with one another and wondering what is happening to the world. There is some solace in the fact that the sunshine is pleasant, the skies are blue, the coffee is good, the cakes are even better and the local brandy, if without the refinement of a good Cognac, is potent and offers one passing moments of cheerful insensibility, but if Celeste's crazy scheme goes through, which is to say, if you add your signature to Gwendoline's, we shall almost certainly be ruined and I shall be unable to afford even those small pleasures which at present keep me sane.

All this, as you may have possibly inferred from my letter, is beginning to tell on my nerves and I am going away for a short stay with Matthew and Nicky in Jerusalem. Could you please write to me care of them, for I fear that Celeste may tamper with the mail in my absence.

Yours ever,
Henry

Dear Berthold,

Et tu, Brute. What has gone wrong with the world, or, more particularly, what has gone wrong with the family? Am I the only sane Hoch alive? Her letter was, no doubt, as you say, 'convincing and businesslike' but have you no sense of responsibility to the actual and potential beneficiaries of the family trust? If you have taken legal advice and feel you are empowered to act in this way, I shall not attempt to stop you, but I fail to understand why everybody should suddenly be overwhelmed with a passion for opera. I know that you are acting out of filial piety and that by lending the money we shall have an opera house named after our late father, but to name an opera house after Father is a little akin to naming a monastery after Henry VIII. Father was tone deaf and the only time he ever set foot in an Opera House was when Celeste and I took him to Glyndebourne on his ninetieth birthday and that, if you will remember, was under the pretext of taking him on a picnic (and he kept grumbling all the way there why anyone should want to wear evening dress for a picnic).

My own feeling is that your usually impeccable judgement has, if I may say so, been upset by the amount of publicity accorded to Celeste. I don't know why papers should have such influence, but the feeling in England seems to be that anyone who has received favourable mention in *The Times* cannot be wrong and cannot do wrong. She can and she does.

In the meantime I am sharing my house with a stranger, and a troublesome stranger at that. I have taken to going to synagogue on weekday evenings, not out of a search for religious solace – though in recent weeks I have been wishing that I was rather more religious than I am – but because the synagogue is a quiet and calm place, attended by calm and sane people, and if they are otherwise their insanity does not take any outward form. The Rabbi gives a Talmud *shiur* and although my Hebrew is bad and my Yiddish non-existent, I pick up stray wisps of knowledge which I find oddly comforting. I have even grown to like and respect the Rabbi, at least in those moments when he confines himself to teaching, for when he draws me aside to point out the errors of Celeste's ways he brings me back to grim earth, and I have to tell him that she is a big girl now and that I am not responsible for her actions. 'But she is your wife,' he protests, 'and the Talmud says that a bad wife you can beat till she becomes good.' To which I replied that Celeste would take a lot of beating. He is, however, satisfied that I am not a party to her sins and as a mark of his favour he has asked for his bowler back.

Perhaps she will change when it is all over, but I rather fear she may get worse. Don't send your wife into politics, Berthold.

Yours in despair,
Henry

Dear Matthew,

I'm afraid I shall not be coming to stay with you and Nicky as I had hoped. I have suffered a slight recurrence of my old bronchial troubles and am feeling poorly. I could have done with a few days away from Bor Shachor and the madhouse it has become, but then it has never been particularly sane in the first place. What is more worrying is the fact that poor old Berthold has gone barmy. The virtual collapse of the company has more or less unhinged his mind and he has virtually signed over the family trust to Celeste who, if you saw her on television last night, shows advanced signs of dementia.

I often wonder at such times why I ever left England, and I suppose part of the answer is that England left me. It was changing so fast from the place I had known and loved that I wanted to get away from it as one wants to get away from the presence of a friend smitten with some incurable plague.

Then, amid atrophying faculties, and atrophying means, there was the prospect of atrophying routine. I was already semi-retired and soon I would be completely retired. People complain of stultifying routines, I loved them. I loved catching the 8.17 to Victoria and then changing onto the District line for Moorgate, and then up three floors on the oak-lined rickety lift with the oval mirror to my office and my almost non-existent mail and dear Miss Petherick waiting with her Venus pencil poised to take my dictation. But there was less and less for me to do and I spent much of my day attempting *The Times* crossword, so I left before I was asked to go. Bor Shachor opened not only new prospects but new challenges, but I'm an Englishman with English ways and am not equipped for the intrigues – part Byzantine, part Galician – which I discovered, but Celeste has taken to them as a duck takes to water.

What a year of calamities this has been, Father dead, the Hall about to be destroyed, the company in ruins, my brother deranged, my wife insane, myself in pieces, my marriage on the rocks. This could never have happened had I remained in Isleworth.

My love to Nicky,

> Yours,
> Henry

Dear Berthold,

I am writing to you by express post in case you should hear this – if indeed you haven't already heard it – from any other source.

I, Henry Horatio Hoch, am in politics! I had no ambitions in that direction, but neither, I should imagine, did Celeste, and I'm beginning to believe that these things come on one unbidden, like some visitation.

I was walking home from synagogue this morning when I heard rapid footsteps behind me and I turned round to find Donegal trotting after me.

'A word with you,' he gasped. We sat down on a bench while he wiped his brow and recovered his breath.

'I keep forgetting that my running days are over, but let me get to the point. I want you to stand for the council.'

'Me?'

'Yes.'

'For the council?'

'Yes.'

'Isn't one lunatic in the family enough?'

'It's partly because she's standing that I want you to stand.'

'For which party?'

'The Holy Alliance, of course. I'd make you number two on the list. You'd be Deputy Mayor if we won, and with you on our list we would win.'

'You're not being serious.'

'I've never been more serious in my life. The idea came to me last night in a vision. Mittwoch was telling me you're hardly out of synagogues these days, that you come to his study group, that you give money to help this unfortunate and that. He couldn't have painted a better picture of you if you'd been St Francis himself, and he asked how is it that the wife of such a man should declare war against God in his Heaven.'

'She hasn't – '

But you know what he means, and I had to explain to him that wives have a will of their own and a life of their own, but then, I thought to myself, so do husbands. What's to stop you from standing in the elections?'

'Me?'

'Yes, you.'

'I'm not a politician.'

'Jaysus, nobody is a politician. You become one if you have to be. Was your wife a politician before she came here? Do you think I was?'

'I don't even subscribe to everything your party stands for,'

'Who does? Do you think your wife subscribes to everything the League stands for? Because apart from anything else they don't know what they stand for themselves. You want to get something done and you join the party through whose agency you are most likely to do it. Join us.'

'My wife would leave me if I did,' I said half-jokingly.

'All the more reason,' he said with a nudge.

Celeste was away for the weekend at some sort of conference in Tel Aviv and Matthew and Nicky were staying with me. I remained silent about it all through lunch, as if harbouring some guilty secret, and once or twice Nicky asked me if anything was wrong, for I hardly ate a thing. After lunch, however, while Nicky was resting and Matthew and I were washing up, I told him about Donegal's offer, thinking he would laugh, but, on the contrary, he took it seriously and thought it was a good idea.

'Astute fellow,' he said, 'you'd be worth four or five thousand votes to them.'

'But I hardly speak Hebrew.'

'You wouldn't have to. All you'd have to do is to sit on their platform with the bowler on your head and a carnation in your button-hole. They all appreciate a gentleman in these parts, especially if he looks like one – there are so few about. Besides which, the Ango-Saxon immigrant is the nearest thing they have to an aristocracy.'

'I thought it was the Russians and their progeny.'

'Been around for too long. People are looking for new faces or, as in your case, an old face in a new setting. Besides, Anglo-Saxons have money and are less likely to put their fingers in the till.'

'And you mean if I stood for the Holy Alliance I would counter the attraction of Celeste?'

'Celeste isn't an attraction, dear boy, she's a deterrent.'

'Celeste?'

'Afraid so. You see, they're largely orientals round here with a firm belief that a woman's place, in so far as she has a place at all, is in the home – '

'What about Golda?'

'Yes, but a Prime Minister is remote, on high, beyond their

reckoning. A woman mayor would be here right on their own door step. They wouldn't care for that.'

That evening I phoned Donegal to accept. He was round at my door ten minutes later with a bottle of Paddy whiskey.

'An occasion like this calls for a drink,' he said. 'You'll live to bless this day, so will Bor Shachor.'

By the next morning, after a sleepless night, however, I was already regretting it and was about to phone Donegal when Celeste appeared.

'I hear you're standing for the council,' she said, peeling a glove off her fingers. 'Good for you – it'll keep you out of mischief.' And it was her tone, amused, patronising, dismissive, which finally made my mind up for me. So here I am, the candidate. I only wish I was happier with my decision than I feel.

Yours,
Henry

Dear Berthold,

Thank you for your congratulations but I'm not sure that I'm entirely happy with the amazement with which you greeted the news. I was – though that was after your time – a fairly frequent speaker at the school debating society, and you yourself said that my after-dinner speeches were always the highlight of the annual staff dinners and that I had 'a feeling for words'.

The election campaign opened formally this morning. I spent much of the day at HQ, being briefed on the plan of campaign and attended my first public meeting this evening in a draughty cinema, smelling of fried onions, urine and disinfectant, though about me on the platform there was an overpowering odour of after-shave, distributed freely by one of my fellow candidates, a Mr Izbicki, who is a manufacturer or importer of chemists' sundries (and a dreadful waste of after-shave it was for half the platform party was bearded). I was in the front row right by Donegal, who made the opening speech and then spoke again by way of introduction to the fourteen or fifteen speakers (or maybe more – I lost count) who followed. Who said we Jews were a hasty, impatient race? I wouldn't say that the audience listened without a murmur. They shuffled, coughed, spluttered, chatted, made loud interjections, and of course they ate, but they remained in their places to the bitter end, as if waiting for some reward. If I was nearly overcome by the after-shave at the beginning of the meeting, I was almost overcome by the speeches before the end, and I would have been but for an interjection from the audience which was obviously directed at me.

Someone – Izbicki, as it happened – was going on about housing problems, when a swarthy figure stood up and shouted – what does your party know about housing, when one of your leading candidates is living in a palace? I speak Hebrew poorly, but I understand it fairly well and I certainly understood that and jumped to my feet.

'I had the good fortune', I said, 'to have been born in a fairly comfortable family, and I don't think one has to apologise for that. I only wish others were as comfortable. My house, it is true, is large. Our house in London was even larger and I was brought up in a house with thirty bedrooms (murmurs of "ooo!"). We have a long tradition of hospitality in our family. We like to entertain and keep open house and we hoped to continue this tradition now that we had made our home in Bor Shachor' – and what is more, I said all that in Hebrew. Donegal gazed at me open-mouthed, but no one was more surprised than myself and I stood slightly dumb-founded while the applause echoed about my ears.

'What do you mean, you don't speak Hebrew?' Donegal said to me later, 'you speak it better than I do.'

'I didn't know I was speaking Hebrew,' I said, 'as a matter of fact I didn't quite realise I was speaking till I had finished.'

These few words had an immediate repercussion, for when I got home at night there were forty or fifty people waiting for admission. They had taken my remarks as an open invitation.

Yours ever,
Henry

TO HIGHAM : HIGHAM MIGHTY : NEW YORK

THANKS MESSAGE OF SUPPORT STOP SECOND ON LIST STOP
HOPEFUL STOP RUMOURS UNFOUNDED STOP HAVE NOT LEFT
WIFE STOP WIFE HAS NOT LEFT ME STOP HENRY

Dear Berthold,

Let me set your mind at rest. Celeste has not left me. The rumours as you say, are ridiculous, but how did they arise? We've had phone calls about it from William and Stanley and a cable from Gerald. Can a husband and wife not have political differences without separating? It is true that Celeste is away from home for days at a time, but she's a national figure and is in demand all over the country as a speaker, which, happily, or unhappily, I am not. When she is here we both rise early, but hardly have a chance to talk, at least not at breakfast, for we eat behind our papers, but then, of course, we did the same in England, the difference now being that we hardly have time to talk even in bed, for she sits up with the pillows propped behind her, cigarette in mouth, her glasses (a slant-eyed pair with heavy black rims, which she must have got in London, but which she's only just started wearing now) halfway down her nose, going over her speeches for the next day, and sometimes half-consciously throwing me a word like : 'Anything exciting happen today?'

And I might say something without looking up from my papers, and she would reply, and we could have an exchange like this for half an hour, without either of us having the slightest idea what the other was saying. One acquires a knack of letting the mouth function without engaging the brain.

Although the Alliance are getting good crowds, they are getting better ones, partly because of the publicity which Celeste generates. One would have thought that a country with a woman Prime Minister would not get that excited about the prospect of a woman mayor, but there we are.

My own style has changed a little, though I am not sure if it has improved. I suspect that Donegal initially wanted me on his platforms merely as a pretty face, but I am now called on to speak three or four times a day.

'You're good,' he told me once, 'very good, for apart from anything else you know when to stop, which these other characters don't, but can I ask you one thing – no under-statement, and no self-deprecatory remarks, for people will always take them at their face value, so don't begin by saying, "I am not an authority on the subject, but", for their imme-diate reaction is that if you are not an authority, what business have you to stand for the council in the first place? In Israel everybody is an authority, certainly everybody who speaks in public or stands for public office. The thing you have to tell yourself before you start is that you are as wise as Solomon, as strong as Samson, as brave as Saul, as far-seeing as Isiah, as patient as Job. *You* don't have to cut yourself down to size, they'll do it for you.'

Pictures of Celeste, looking a little schoolmarmish and severe, stare out at one from every paper and there are large portraits of her, Abba and Humphry gazing down from every hoarding. Not a few posters have been defaced. Abba has been given gaps in his teeth and Celeste a beard and mous-tache. The portraits of Humphry, however, have been left severely alone : no defacer could improve on nature.

There are a few posters of me in a bowler hat (Donegal insisted on that), and I see that on one of the posters, someone has affixed horns to both sides of my hat. What is the signi-ficance in that?

There are larger than life portraits of Donegal standing amid the skyscrapers of his new paradise, inviting Bor Shachor to follow the Holy Alliance into the twentieth century. There are something like twelve different parties contesting the elections. There is no more Kung Fu to be seen in the cinemas, nor even Fu King; they have all been booked solid for public meetings. Donegal is making much out of the fact that Celeste, whose efforts have delayed the start of the tower-block city, should now be heading the Workers' League, which itself claims to be committed to tower blocks. Tower blocks are every-where in the air, and each party is seeking to out-storey the other. Donegal's plans call for twenty-two-storey blocks.

Other parties call for thirty, forty, and even fifty storeys. One party, or at least one party leader, has demanded an erection taller than the Empire State Building, which would shine out across the world, in fulfilment of the prophetic promise that 'thou shalt be a light unto the nations'. In one way or another Bor Shachor has been placed firmly on the map as the Eatanswille of Israel and it has become a tourist attraction. Taxis and air-conditioned buses unload whole shoals of Americans in funny hats and elongated shorts, who rush hither and thither among the crowds taking photos, and one fat gentleman with hairy knees has been going round handing out cigars as if he was a candidate. There is something like a gala atmosphere in the town and the general air of conviviality reminds me a little of the VE-day celebrations in Fetlock.

People stop me in the streets for my autograph, or to take pictures beside me 'for the folks back home'.

I have, of course, had to forsake all my old haunts like Kapulski's and Steinmatzky's, and most of my old friends, and I hardly have time to eat. Donegal has urged me to keep a diary. 'You and I are making history,' he said, 'it'll be worth a fortune to your grandchildren,' but I feel that my grandchildren are sufficiently provided for as it is. My own relaxation are these letters to you, and perhaps you may wish to hold on to them.

Yours ever,
Henry

Dear Rodney,

Thank you for your letter, the first, I believe, since we left England.

Yes, it is true that I am standing for the local council. It is further true that I am a candidate for something called the 'Holy Alliance'.

My knowledge of history is not, I'm afraid, as extensive as yours, but if, as you tell me, 'the Tsar of all the Russias headed a Holy Alliance to keep Europe in thraldom', I'm prepared to take your word for it, but I think I am right in believing that there is no connection between his Holy Alliance and ours.

I am nevertheless grateful for your good wishes.

> Your loving father,
> Henry

Dear Berthold,

Five days to the poll and all's ill, or at least Donegal is and his wife says I'm killing him.

It began with a reply I gave to a question that, while I was against allowing public transport to desecrate the Sabbath, the present law meant that the rich, with cars, could travel, while the poor, without, could not. Such matters, I felt, were better settled by example than compulsion, and that if the non-observant could see the joy one can derive from observance, they too would, in time, begin to keep the Sabbath. Compulsion, I said – in what I thought was an inspired peroration – makes enemies; examples win friends.

The press, of course, misconstrued my remarks as the press will, and the following morning there were headlines everywhere, exclaiming that a Holy Alliance candidate was in favour of public transport on the Sabbath – which, by the way, is the first time I've made the headlines since the blessed campaign began.

Donegal came upon me while I was still at breakfast with a purple face and quivering hands.

'Are you trying to undermine the party?' he demanded.

'No, but the papers obviously are.'

'You will have to publish a disclaimer saying that you are categorically against public transport on Shabbat.'

'That is not my position.'

'It's the position of the party.'

'Then the party is wrong.'

'You've found a fine time to say so – five days before the poll.'

'Nobody asked me before.'

'I thought you cherished Shabbat.'

'I do.'

'And that you were an Orthodox Jew.'

'I am, which doesn't mean that I'm prepared to ram Orthodoxy down the throats of those who are not. I am perfectly willing to publish a correction, but not on the lines you suggest.'

'Then we're finished,' he said in a broken voice, 'that's just what the ultras have been praying for. They're already preparing handbills to show that the Holy Alliance is unholy, that it does not believe in the Sabbath. We'll be torn apart. They'll grab one part of our vote, the League the other. Everything I've worked for and hoped for is done for. We're finished.

He turned to go, but he seemed so broken that I rushed after him and put an arm round his shoulder.

'Look,' I said, 'let's talk about it. You probably haven't had breakfast – have you?'

'Who wants breakfast? Who can eat?'

'A cup of coffee.'

He came back into the kitchen and sat down beside me on a high stool in the dining area.

'You don't look well,' I said.

'I'll feel better when I've read your disclaimer.'

'Surely you don't expect me to write something I don't mean.'

'No, but I expect you to write something you should mean,' and we finally worked out a compromise in which I said that while it was always better to spread Judaism by example, one could not have public bodies, like the bus co-operative, desecrating the Sabbath.

An hour later Donegal was on the phone to me.

'I've read it through to head office, and they don't like it.'

'Well, they can lump it,' I said, and put the phone down.

I had hardly disposed of that when Celeste came downstairs carrying a small suitcase.

'Going somewhere?' I said.

'You know very well I am, I told you earlier in the week.'

'When?'

'Monday night.'

'I couldn't have been listening.'

'I thought you weren't, that's why I told you again on Tuesday. You'll find everything you need in the fridge.'

'You mean you'll be away over Shabbat?'

'I told you I would be. I suggested you might want to eat with Gwendoline, but you said you'd rather not. There's a roast turkey in the fridge and some salads. I must rush.'

'I'd rather you didn't.'

'Henry, you're not trying to interfere in my election campaign?'

'Have you ever known me to interfere?'

'Not so far.'

'I don't care to be on my own on Shabbat.'

'I've been away before.'

'I wasn't happy about it then, to be honest, and I shouldn't like you to make a habit of it.'

'I'm not making a habit of it, for God's sake, the campaign's nearly over. I have a major commitment in Tel Aviv.'

'You have a prior commitment here.'

'This is going to upset a great many arrangements.'

'I'm sorry.'

'You might have mentioned it earlier in the week.'

'You didn't ask me earlier in the week.'

'Henry, I told you – '

'But you didn't *ask*.'

She sighed, took off her coat and her gloves and remained. We had, I'm afraid, a rather chilly Sabbath, which was only partly due to the fact that the cold turkey and salads were still half-frozen. She obviously felt that while I had been entirely within my rights, I hadn't been quite sporting.

We ate the evening meal in silence but as we were clearing up she said to me :

'You've changed, you know.'

'For better or worse?'

'All changes are for the worse in people of our age. It means that on top of other faults, one acquires the fault of inconsistency.'

Yours ever,
Henry

Dear Stanley and Elaine,

Thank you for your unexpected letter.

'I'm sorry you've not been able to contact us on the phone. The phone is in perfect working order, and so – I hasten to add – are we, but the campaign is at its height and we're hardly ever at home.

Trends seem to be running in favour of your mother's party, but it's only four days to the poll and by the time you get this letter you should know the worst (or the best), and if you won't have a mother as a mayor, you may have a father as deputy mayor.

My love to Jason and Jeremy.

Your loving father,
Henry

Dear Berthold,

Eve of the poll. We have had our last meeting and I have made my last speech, and I have retired exhausted to an empty house to get some much-needed sleep, but sleep I can't. The phone was ringing as I entered. I tried to ignore it, but it persisted and, behold, it was Stanley phoning from London, and choking with rage. 'If you can't run for public office without forgetting the names of your grandchildren, then you shouldn't be running for public office,' he shouted. I had asked him to give my love to Jeremy and Jason (who are, of course, William's boys), which I would have thought is a forgivable error to make at the end of an exhausting week, but he (and Elaine, who was too furious even to talk to me) obviously did not, and I spent the better part of half an hour (and I suppose the better part of £50) in apologies.

We have had an energetic campaign, but I am not too hopeful of the outcome. I finally caved in to Donegal's demands that I publish the disclaimer he wanted, because he seemed in imminent danger of caving in himself. He is our biggest electoral asset, an able speaker, a frantic organiser, who has done many small favours to many small people who, however, have exactly the same vote as big people, and he has a large personal following. He has been ill throughout the campaign, a fact which he tried to keep to himself, without much success, and which we have since kept to ourselves and he has, ill health or not, completed the full programme of hustings. Yesterday he seemed so unwell, with yellow patches round his eyes in an otherwise scarlet face, that we begged him to stay in bed, but he insisted on getting up, and fortified himself with large swigs of Irish whiskey.

'It's me last bottle,' he said, 'when that's gone I'll be gone.'

We had the dinner in his house before the final rally and he seemed so lively, hopeful and expansive that I lost the slight feeling of foreboding with which I came to the meal.

'We're winning,' he said, 'I can feel it in my bones.'

'It could be the rheumatics,' said Izbicki.

'It's Jewish good sense asserting itself,' said Donegal. 'What I couldn't do for this place if I had an outright majority.'

'You're not expecting one, surely,' I said.

'No, but I deserve one. This is the best campaign I've ever fought, with the best team. We'll beat the League, that's for sure.'

'I find that hard to believe.'

'That's your Englishness, belief comes hard to the English. We'll win, not with an overall majority, but we'll win, and Rafi expects me to win, that's why he stepped down. He wasn't making way for your wife out of gentleman's courtesy. He's an old pro and knows when the going is bad. And what's more, there were many things he wanted to do for Bor Shachor, but he couldn't because he had his left-wingers breathing down his neck. Now, of course, he can let me do them, with the necessary show of opposition, and blame it all on me. He doesn't breathe without calculation, that fella, but one thing he did miscalculate. He thinks that after the Holy Alliance's been in office for four years the electorate will be cured of religion for good and will be only too glad to get back to the League. There he's mistaken. Once we're in, we're in to stay. I shall find new homes, new jobs, I shall open new schools and colleges, I shall give the place a new standing and new image. To most minds, even to ours, religion means incompetence, I will show that it can work, that God's will can be done on earth as it is in Heaven – '

'And give us this day our daily bread,' I muttered under my breath.

He was in splendid form at the rally and was on his feet for over an hour. His speech, a mixture of prophetic declamation and Irish blarney, was cheered and applauded at every pause.

'They'd better stop cheering,' Izbicki whispered out of the side of his mouth, 'or he'll go on forever.' For my part I hoped that he would, for I was to follow and I was painfully aware that after such a performance anything I might have to say would be an anti-climax. Just then his voice faded. He swayed slightly, grasped the table to steady himself, and with a gasp fell forward on his face.

There was immediate pandemonium with men shouting, women shrieking and people dashing in all directions.

I made the mistake of shouting 'Is there a doctor in the house?' There were a dozen. One was a cardiologist, another an endocrinologist, a third a dermatologist, etc. and they had a conference over his prostrate little figure before deciding that he was probably the cardiologist's pigeon. An ambulance, however, was by then on the scene and he was passed over the heads of the milling crowds to the waiting vehicle.

I have just returned from the hospital and the doctor thinks that given a complete rest he should make a good recovery, but as far as our electoral chances are concerned the damage has been done. His collapse is now public knowledge and in Bor Shachor the Holy Alliance is Donegal and Donegal is the Holy Alliance and I cannot see us getting many votes without him.

Still one plays for the game and not for the victory. It was a good fight and I feel the better for it.

Yours ever,
Henry

Dear Berthold,

Thank you for your cable. As Celeste says I've been and gone and done it, though it was dear little Donegal who did it for us. He died an hour or two after being admitted to hospital. Nothing in his life was quite as dramatic as his leaving of it. The news was broadcast on every bulletin throughout the day and we were swept into office on a wave of sympathy. We got ten seats against the eight of the Workers' League and the six won by the rest of the parties put together, and with poor Donegal out of the way, of course, I am the mayor.

I say this with less jubilation than dismay, and it reminds me a little of the day I proposed to Celeste for, according to her, my proposal went something like this :

'Will you marry me?'

'Yes.'

'You will?'

'Yes.'

'Good God.'

That's how I feel now, though if my mayoralty should prove no worse than my marriage, I shall be fairly satisfied and so, will Bor Shachor – I think.

Yours ever,

Henry

Ts